JUST LAST YEAR a powerful Druid spell flung Fiona and Bran McCool back in time two thousand years to ancient Ireland. There they found a friend in Finn, the young warrior who holds the key to the mystery of their unknown father. But when the McCools call on the spell to return them to the scene of that first adventure, Bran's magic goes wild and they find themselves in the wrong place in time.

The unpredictable spell has brought them to the Ireland of 839 A.D.—to a land of art and learning, a land constantly threatened by Outsiders from the north who may invade at any moment. In this strange but amazing place, Fiona and Bran are caught up in the wonders of a life so old but yet so new to them that they nearly lose sight of their mission to find Finn.

Finally, on a magic night, to the haunting chant of a powerful Druid, Old Biddy Gwynn, the two travelers are transformed into ravens and sent flying into a lost chapter from the Legend of Finn.

Through ravens' eyes, Bran and Fiona peer into the secrets of the McCool history and see the beautiful, strangely familiar red doe together with the astonishing image of their father. Gradually, they understand the truth that they have always known about themselves but could only realize through this journey of discovery. The masterful telling of two children's quest for a past brimming with wonder and magic is Mary Tannen's exciting sequel to *The Wizard Children of Finn.*

THE
LOST LEGEND
OF FINN

BY MARY TANNEN

Alfred A. Knopf
NEW YORK

THIS IS A BORZOI BOOK
PUBLISHED BY ALFRED A. KNOPF, INC.

Library of Congress Cataloging in Publication Data
Tannen, Mary. The lost legend of Finn.
Summary: Determined to find out the truth about
their father, Bran and Fiona use their uncle's magic
book and go back in time to ninth-century Ireland.
Sequel to "The Wizard Children of Finn."
[1. Space and time—Fiction. 2. Celts—Fiction.
3. Ireland—Fiction] I. Title.
PZ7.T1617Lo 1982   [Fic]   81-15599
ISBN 0-394-85211-7   AACR2
ISBN 0-394-95211-1 (lib. bdg.)

Manufactured in the United States of America
2 4 6 8 0 9 7 5 3 1

To Michael

THE LOST LEGEND
OF FINN

1

"Shut up out there!"

"Bran, shhh!"

"How's a guy supposed to do long division with all that noise?"

"You are in a theater, you know, not a library. The library is the big building with the lions out in front."

"I know where I am, Fiona. I just want to know why the audience always has to be so loud when I'm doing my math."

"Maybe they don't know this is the night you do your math," said Fiona, eyeing her mother's stage make-up. "We should put a note in the playbill: 'Please refrain from laughing and applauding during the Thursday evening performance, as Bran McCool's math homework is due on Friday.'"

Bran glared at his sister who was smiling at herself in the mirror. "You crack me up. You're so funny you should be on TV so I could turn you off. Funny-looking, too," he added.

Fiona stuck out her tongue. Bran went back to his homework. Another explosion of laughter shook the flimsy dressing room walls. Bran threw down his pencil and put his head in his hands.

"Why don't you tell your teacher you couldn't do your work because the audience was too loud?" Fiona tried to be helpful now. "She'll understand. They let you off easy in fourth grade. It's not like seventh."

"I don't want everyone to know that Ma makes us sit in her dressing room every night while she's on stage," sputtered Bran. "It's weird. Why can't she let us stay home alone? We're old enough."

Fiona's hand circled over a big gold box of candy and lit upon a champagne truffle. She popped the candy into her mouth. "You know why," she mumbled. She offered the candy to her brother.

Bran shook his head and took an apple from the fruit bowl instead. Fiona tried to pry the champagne truffle off her back molar. Bran chomped on his apple and went back to his math problems.

Fiona did know why Sadie was holding them prisoner in her dressing room. She knew only too well.

It had been a year since she and her brother had returned from their trip through time to ancient Ireland. It had been hard enough to get Bran to come home with her then. If Finn hadn't told Bran to go, he would still be there.

They hadn't been home long when Fiona realized she had brought only part of Bran back with her. His heart was still with Finn and his band of warriors, the Fianna. That's why he didn't eat candy anymore—Bran who used to be the biggest junk-food freak of all. He was staying in shape to go back and rejoin Finn and the Fianna.

That's why Bran had taken up fencing instead of soccer in school this year. Fiona nibbled at the edge of a chocolate-covered cherry. That's why Sadie wouldn't let them out of her sight if she could help it. She was afraid they would somehow find a way to go back to Finn. Fiona had tried to reassure her mother that she, for one, was perfectly content to remain in the good old twentieth century, but she couldn't blame Sadie for being nervous.

More great guffaws came from the audience. "She's hot tonight," remarked Fiona.

"I give up."

"Do your social studies," suggested Fiona. "It doesn't take as much thinking."

Bran shoved his math book to one side and opened his looseleaf notebook. "Oh, brother!"

"Now what's the matter?"

"I forgot. We're studying family trees. I gotta have my father's name, when he was born, his occupation—"

"So what?"

"So nothing, except we don't know anything about our father. He could have been the sandman or Santa Claus or—"

"I had the same homework when I was in fourth grade," said Fiona airily.

"So, what did *you* say?"

Fiona hesitated, then decided against another champagne truffle. "I think I said his name was Dooley. Yeah. That was it. Dr. Dooley McCool. I said he was a scientist and he lived in the Okefenokee Swamp."

"How do you spell Okefenokee?"

"Got me. I don't even know where it is."

"I have an idea. I'll tell Ma I need it for my homework, and maybe she'll tell me about my dad."

"It must be nice to be so young and innocent," sighed Fiona.

"Did you ever just ask her? Straight out?"

Fiona set the candy box on the floor and sauntered back over to where Sadie's makeup was strewn over the counter. "Yeah, I asked her." She took out a tissue and wiped the chocolate from her mouth. "I used to ask her a lot. I asked her in the morning before she was really awake. I asked her at night when she came to tuck me in. I asked her when the oatmeal boiled over and every time she dropped a plate. I asked her when she was on the phone with her agent. For a while I was asking her two or three times a day."

"Did she ever say anything?"

"Nothing. Except that he died in a war long ago. And that she didn't change her name when she got married because she liked the name McCool and she was used to it, or something like that. So you can ask her if you want, but I don't think she'll tell you anything."

Fiona sucked in her cheeks and dabbed some of Sadie's rouge on her cheekbones. "I used to be so crazy to find out something about our dad that I used to sit on the top of the stairs in Uncle Rupert's house and try to imagine his ghost walking down the hall." She laughed.

"Did you ever see him?"

"Nope. I got so I could see our grandparents, and Great-grandma McCool, but never our dad. I figured he never lived there. His ghost must be haunting whatever battlefield he died on."

Bran's eyes grew big and dark. "Did you ever try it on Halloween night?"

"Why should I try on Halloween?"

"Halloween was a magic night back in Ireland. *Samhain*. Remember? The hills opened up so the spirits could walk around, and normal people hid indoors—"

As if Fiona could ever forget *Samhain* in Ireland! "So what's your point?"

"Just that! If Halloween was magic back then, maybe

some of the magic has lasted up until now. And maybe if we went to Uncle Rupert's house on Halloween, we could see our dad's ghost."

"But Halloween's Saturday," protested Fiona. "I was going to dress Punk and go trick or treating."

"We can go trick or treating up there, in Perry, and look for the ghost, too," argued Bran.

Fiona stuck her finger into a jar of lavender cream eye shadow and smeared it on her lids. "Do you think Ma is going to let us go up and visit Uncle Rupert, of all people, on one of the four magic nights of ancient Ireland?"

Bran took a jump shot and sunk his apple core into the wastebasket. "Of course she's not going to let us. We'll have to lie, that's all."

"Lie? To Ma?"

"She hasn't been exactly straight with us, has she? Look, Fiona, I didn't just think about our father now because it's in my homework. I've been dreaming about him. Sometimes I think I see him out of the corner of my eye, and when I try to look right at him, he disappears."

Fiona felt a little shiver go up her spine. She had had those dreams, too, a while ago. But she didn't have them anymore. For some reason Fiona had forgotten, up until this conversation with Bran, how much she had always thought and wondered about her father.

"I've outgrown it," she told herself as she brushed on some navy-blue mascara. But way deep down, she knew that wasn't true. Something had scared her, frightened her from asking any more questions. Maybe she had come too close. Fiona shook the thought from her mind and added another coat of mascara. She batted her eyes at her brother.

"How do I look?"

"Neat! You look like one of those baby birds with the big purple eyes that fall out of their nests in the spring, before they get their feathers—" Bran ducked to avoid a sponge sailing by his ear.

"How about it?" he challenged. "Are you going up to Uncle Rupert's with me, or are you too scared?"

Fiona outlined her lips in red pencil. "Why should I be scared? I don't even believe in ghosts anymore."

"If you won't come, that proves you're scared."

"Little brothers are so tiresome," Fiona sighed, scanning Sadie's collection of lipsticks. "O.K., I guess it's no big deal to go up to Uncle Rupert's and look for a ghost. But don't be disappointed if he doesn't appear."

The audience roared and clapped.

"Curtain call," announced Fiona. "Make sure you get up a little earlier tomorrow. I'll have a plan ready by then on how we're going to get to Perry without Ma finding out." She filled in her lips with magenta lipstick and pouted into the mirror.

"Eeee-ah!"

Fiona whirled around to see her mother swooning dramatically in the doorway.

"That face! You scared me out of ten years' growth." Sadie handed her a box of tissues and a big jar of Albolene Cream. "Start wiping," she ordered.

2

So?" Bran mocked Fiona over his bowl of 7-Grains Natural Cereal the next morning. "What's the plan?"

"The plan is," Fiona stalled, fussing over her Pop-Tart, which was stuck in the toaster. "The plan is—" The truth was that she hadn't been able to come up with just the right plan.

Saved by the bell. Fiona picked up the phone. It was Madeline Morgan, Sadie's closest friend, calling to invite Fiona and Bran to the country with her family for the weekend. Madeline had two children, Jessica and Peter, who were about the same ages as Fiona and Bran, and she often invited the McCools when Sadie was working. Fiona and Bran usually went, even though Jessica had a tendency to be bossy and Bran sometimes suspected

Peter of wetting his pants. Anything was better than playing Monopoly all Saturday and Sunday in Sadie's dressing room. This time Fiona politely declined, saying that she and Bran had made other plans.

"Who was on the phone?" asked Sadie, coming in as Fiona hung up.

Fiona studied her mother with interest. She could never be sure what Sadie would look like on any given morning. She could have her hair stuffed into a baseball cap, looking like the boy who delivered the groceries, or she could be dressed for an early appointment and be a dead ringer for a visiting countess. Today Sadie was wearing her red hair in a pony tail almost on top of her head. She had wrapped herself in an embroidered Chinese silk robe. "Woody Woodpecker meets Fu Manchu," decided Fiona.

"That was Maddy." Fiona finally retrieved her Pop-Tart from the toaster. "She wants me 'n' Bran to go to the country with her this weekend."

"That's nice. I'll call her back later." Sadie took her teacup to the table and hunched over it, letting the steam rise to her face.

"She said she was going out and wouldn't be back until late tonight." Fiona thought fast. "We're supposed to be down in the lobby early tomorrow morning, and they'll come by and pick us up." She shot Bran a glance that clearly said, "Shut up. I'll explain later."

"O.K. Wake me, if I'm not up before you go."

Fiona looked uncomfortable.

"Ma," said Bran, putting his lunch, a tahini on whole grain sandwich, into his backpack, "I forgot to ask you this for social studies. What was my father's name, where was he born, and what was his occupation?"

Sadie choked on her tea. Fiona handed her a napkin.

"What kind of question is that for social studies?" she protested, mopping the tea off her robe. "When I was in fourth grade we studied Pygmies and Eskimos and stuff."

"We're studying our families," said Bran. "And all the kids know about their fathers. Even Richie whose dad lives in California. They all know about their dads."

Bran sat down next to Sadie. "Ma, it's not just for social studies that I need to know. I've been thinking about it a lot, and not knowing him makes me feel like I'm only half there. You know what I mean?"

Sadie bit her lower lip and ruffled her son's blond hair. "Yeah," she said softly. "And I wish I could tell you. I wish I could just say, 'His name is Dooley and he's down in the Okefenokee Swamp.'" She winked at Fiona. "But it ain't that simple, baby. I'm afraid it's something you have to find out for yourself, and I don't think you're old enough for that yet—"

"What about me, Ma? I'm twelve!" piped up Fiona.

Sadie smiled and shook her head. "Not even twelve is old enough, I'm afraid."

"What is it, like an X-rated movie?" countered Fiona. "Do we have to be eighteen or something?"

Sadie straightened up and finished her tea. "When you're old enough, you'll find him."

The McCools let loose with protests, questions, and threats, but Sadie held firm. They were going to be late for school. She'd said all she was going to say, and that was that.

"It's not really lying," said Bran quietly to Fiona over his cereal bowl early the next morning. He knew Fiona's plan now and hoped she wouldn't chicken out.

"I mean, she practically gave us permission, saying when we were old enough, we'd find out for ourselves," Bran added. "Well, I feel old enough."

"Yeah, but—" Fiona popped open a small can of Roller Coasters. "She probably meant we should find out by sending for our birth certificates, not by trying to get his ghost to come out."

"If we were from a normal family, I'd say you were right," said Bran. "But it's not exactly normal to have a mom who makes a mystery out of who your dad is. And, you know, it's not exactly normal to be able to go back two thousand years in time either."

"That was a mistake," Fiona said quickly. "We got mixed up in a Druid chant, that's all. It could have happened to anyone."

Bran raised his eyebrows. "Maybe. Hey, if it makes you feel more normal, you can interview Uncle Rupert while we're there. He was Ma's guardian when she was a teen-ager. He probably knows the whole thing, but no one ever bothered to ask him."

"That's a great idea." Fiona brightened. "I just bought a new notebook at Baronet's."

Fiona went to get her notebook, a spiral-bound one with shiny red covers. Now that she thought about it, she realized they hadn't seen Uncle Rupert since Easter. True, they'd been out of town all summer with the show, but you'd think he would have come into the city for the opening. He was Sadie's uncle and her only living relative, aside from them.

"Did you call Uncle Rupert and tell him we're coming?" asked Fiona, returning with her notebook.

"No. You never know with Uncle Rupert. He could spill the beans to Ma. So I took the key to the front door, in case he's not there," said Bran.

"Out of Ma's jewelry box—" Fiona began to protest.

"Ma told us we had to find our dad for ourselves. I figure from here on, anything's fair." Bran considered for a moment. "Short of murder and grand larceny."

Fiona zipped up her down jacket. What made her

think there was something more involved here than a secret trip to Perry, New York, to visit their great uncle and look for a ghost? She followed Bran out the door and closed it quietly behind her.

When Sadie was working and feeling rich, she hired a limousine and driver to take her and her children up to Uncle Rupert's house. More often, they all took the bus. It dropped them off right in Perry and it was only a five minute walk to the McCool mansion. For that reason, the McCools had no trouble finding their bus at Port Authority Terminal. The only painful part was having to use their savings to purchase the round-trip tickets.

It was a dismal, windy day and the McCools, who had been up late the night before waiting for Sadie's play to be over, fell asleep before the bus left the city limits. Luckily, the driver remembered that the two sleeping children in the back had tickets for Perry, New York, and he shook them awake at their stop.

The McCools stumbled off the bus. As usual, the air smelled colder and cleaner than in New York City. Fiona looked down the broad empty main street of Perry.

"It's been a long time since we've been here," she whispered.

"Yeah." Bran forced himself to talk. "Uncle Rupert's going to be surprised to see us."

The McCools turned into the driveway to the Mc-Cool mansion and almost fell over a silver maple tree.

"Oh, wow! There must have been a storm here last night!" cried Bran.

"I don't think it was last night," said Fiona, grabbing her brother by his sleeve. "Look."

Bran tore his eyes from the fallen tree and followed the direction of his sister's gaze. What had once been a rolling lawn in front of the McCool mansion was a field of hip-high grass, gone brown in the fall. Some thistles, as tall as the McCools, poked arrogantly through the cracked blacktop driveway. The McCool mansion, adrift in this desolation, wept a green shutter in self-pity.

"Something must have happened to Uncle Rupert," said Fiona. "We'd better go down to the bus terminal and call Ma."

"Hold on a minute," objected Bran, jerking his sleeve from Fiona's grasp. "There's something funny here. A lot of people in town know Uncle Rupert and Ma. Someone must have called Ma when this first started happening. I mean, it looks like nobody touched the place all summer."

"But Ma would have told us," said Fiona.

"Unless she wanted to hide it from us," a crafty light came into Bran's eyes. "Unless Uncle Rupert went some-place and she was afraid to tell us where he went."

"Why would she be afraid?" asked Fiona. "Where

would he go that Ma wouldn't want us to know about?"

Bran smiled. "You know where."

A picture suddenly flashed through Fiona's mind of Uncle Rupert on the morning they came back from their adventure to ancient Ireland. He had leaned across the table, his eyes dancing behind his thick lenses, and said to Sadie, "I wonder if *I* could make such a journey."

"But how could he?" whispered Fiona.

"He has the magic book, doesn't he? It's his," reasoned Bran.

"Yeah, but the Druid chant. . . ." Fiona reminded her brother. "He doesn't know the Druid chant."

"How do we know he doesn't know?" asked Bran. "He teaches all that Irish myth and stuff in college. He could have picked up the chant from any of those old books in his library. Maybe it's in the magic book. How would we know? We never could figure out those pointy letters."

"I think we should go home right away," said Fiona. "And tell Ma we were up here, and demand that she tell us—"

"And she'll tell us to figure it out for ourselves when we're old enough," said Bran. "So let's not waste our bus fare. Let's figure it out now." He stalked off toward the house.

They pounded on the door just in case. No one was home.

3

Fiona did not like the way things were going. Purely on principle, she tried never to let her little brother take charge of a situation. He was the one who had wanted to go to Uncle Rupert's, and Fiona had even helped him work out the plan. Now she realized what a terrible mistake she had made. Letting Bran go to Uncle Rupert's, the place where their adventures with Finn had first begun, was like giving a pyromaniac a book of matches. She'd better call Sadie from the house and warn her about what had happened.

Fiona snatched the key from Bran's hand. "I'll open the door."

She swung it open authoritatively, but she couldn't help hesitating on the doorsill. There were forty rooms in the big old house where Sadie, and before her, Uncle

Rupert, had grown up. Even when all the lights were on and everyone was talking at once, there was still a feeling of ghosts lingering in unused rooms.

Bran prodded her from behind. Trying to remember to breathe, Fiona tiptoed toward the library. Bran didn't have to ask why she chose that room first. Together, they went straight to the glass-fronted case where the magic book was kept.

Standing shoulder to shoulder across the entire shelf, as if they had every right to be there, as if the magic book had never existed at all, were the complete works of Sir Walter Scott.

Fiona leaned back against Uncle Rupert's desk, trying to act casual, although her knees were shaking. "Just because it isn't in its case doesn't mean Uncle Rupert chanted himself back to ancient Ireland," she squeaked. "Ahem," Fiona cleared her throat. "After all," she continued in something like her normal voice, "there must be hundreds of books in this room."

Bran said nothing. He was humming a tune through his teeth.

"I'll do the top three rows. You look through the bottom ones," Fiona commanded, pushing the library steps against the shelves.

Half an hour later, she sat down on the top step, exhausted. "I suppose you won't be happy until we search the whole house, will you?"

Bran shook his head.

"Will you stop that silly humming?" said Fiona as Bran trailed after her into the parlor. "It's getting on my nerves."

The other rooms were dusty, but in order. Uncle Rupert's clothes were hanging neatly in one closet. His brown-leather luggage was resting quietly in another. When Bran saw the suitcases he began humming through his teeth again. He followed Fiona down the back stairway into the kitchen.

"Ah ha!" he cried, in his famous detective voice. Hanging on a peg by the door was an old tweed hat. Bran snatched it up and twirled it on his fingers.

"Now why would Uncle Rupert go away without his hat, the hat that he wears everywhere?" Bran asked in the kind of voice that meant he knew the answer and that he knew Fiona knew it, too.

Fiona, refusing to play, merely glared at her brother.

"Uncle Rupert leaves town without his hat, without his luggage. The *only* thing he takes is his magic book. Why? Because he didn't go on any ordinary trip. He went on a trip *back through time* to ancient Ireland!" He tossed the hat back on the hook and gave Fiona a smug little smile.

Fiona stared at the tweed hat. "It just doesn't make sense," she said finally. "Why would a grown man want to go back two thousand years, before they had bathrooms and showers?"

Bran snorted from the pantry where he was rummaging through the canned goods. Fiona hadn't been overly concerned with showers last year in ancient Ireland.

"I know why he went." Bran pried open a jar of baked beans. "I'd go in a minute if I could. I'm just mad he didn't take me."

"I don't know," said Fiona, dipping into a can of cling peaches. "He's too old, and soft, and white. He has arthritis, and if he loses his glasses, he can't see three feet in front of him. He's too—"

Fiona broke off and ran to the window.

"What's the matter?" asked Bran.

"Nothing. I just thought I saw a deer on the lawn. I never remember seeing one out there before."

"Probably all kinds of animals come down from the woods now, with no one living in the house," said Bran.

He threw the jar into the clean and empty garbage can. "I'm going up to the cave."

"Wait!" cried Fiona, not sure she wanted to go up to the cave with Bran, but definitely certain that she didn't want to stay in the house alone. "What do you expect to find in the cave?"

"That's where *we* left from when we went with Finn," said Bran, "so that's probably where Uncle Rupert left from."

"It's not like a bus terminal, you know."

"A cave's a magic place," explained Bran, "half in

the ground and half out of it. Like the magic nights in Ireland were half in one season and half in another."

"Gee, Bran, you sure do know a lot."

Bran shrugged off her sarcasm and left by the kitchen door.

Fiona picked up the phone. Dead. Uncle Rupert must have disconnected it, or maybe when the tree fell— Fiona, wishing with all her heart that they had never left the city, hurried after her brother.

4

I don't think Uncle Rupert ever went into the woods. I don't think he could even climb up to the cave with his arthritis," argued Fiona, wading through the high grass.

Bran skirted the swimming pool and plunged into the woods. "If you don't want to come with me, don't. I know the way."

Fiona had no doubt that Bran knew the way. She had discovered his uncanny sense of direction on their journey with Finn. Still in all, this hardly seemed right. She winced at the dry creaking of branches in the wind.

"If this is right, Bran, how come none of it looks familiar?"

"Does that look familiar?" Bran pointed to an oak tree up ahead. Enough of the leaves had fallen to reveal a tattered woven platform fastened onto the broad branches. The remains of another platform were visible above.

"Finn's tree house," breathed Fiona. Suddenly she was flooded with memories of Finn, the way his hair fell over one eye, the feel of his hand, the way his lips curled into a smile.

"You know," she said wistfully. "It would be nice to see Finn again."

Bran only nodded and continued on the path, past the tree house. Hadn't he been thinking about Finn for a whole year now? Not an hour went by when he didn't long to be with him, while all Fiona ever thought about was having lunch at Burger King with her friends and giggling about boys. Now all of a sudden, *she* thought it would be "nice" to see Finn!

The tree house had brought it all back to Fiona. She vividly recalled the night she and Bran had followed Finn's signs to the cave where he was preparing to go back to ancient Ireland to begin the trials that would turn him from a boy into a man. She remembered his delighted grin when he realized the McCools had somehow been swept up by the Druid chant and carried back with him. Then he had generously invited them along on his journey across Ireland. She smiled to think of how he had asked her, Fiona, a mere eleven-year-old at the time, to be his poet and record his heroic deeds. Sometimes when her friends were bragging about their boyfriends, Fiona wished she could tell them about Finn. But Finn wasn't her boyfriend. He was something more, and better.

"Is this the cave?" asked Fiona as they stopped in front of a hole in the rocky hillside.

"How many caves do you think there are up here?" asked Bran.

"It looks so ordinary."

"Everything looks more ordinary in the daylight. Let's check it out."

The cave did look small and ordinary without the Druid fire and the dancing shadows. But there was the flat rock in the center where Uncle Rupert's magic book had lain.

"The book's not here," observed Fiona.

"Obviously," said Bran. "That just proves Uncle Rupert made the trip. The book went with us on our trip, so it must have gone with him."

Fiona boosted herself up on the rock. Finn had explained that the book was a link between him and them because it was about his adventures, but it belonged to them. Or to Uncle Rupert, who was the actual owner.

"Ha! I found Uncle Rupert's fire!" Bran had been pushing aside the drifts of leaves that covered the floor of the cave.

"How do you know it's Uncle Rupert's and not the same one we had with Finn?"

"Because it's in a different place," said Bran. "And because some of the wood was green and didn't burn. Finn never would have used green wood."

"What are you looking for now?" asked Fiona as Bran began pushing the leaves to the mouth of the cave.

"More clues. You could help me out, you know, instead of sitting there like the great I-am of Siam."

Fiona reluctantly slid off her rock. "Ouch." She twisted her ankle on something hard buried in the leaves.

"You tripped on something?" Bran asked sharply.

"Just a stone, or a log, or . . ."

Bran was already scooping away the leaves at her feet, revealing a large leather-bound volume with heavy parchment pages. He set it on the rock, tenderly wiping away the dirt with his sleeve.

Fiona stared at the ancient book. For a moment, she had the spooky feeling that *it* had been looking for *them*, instead of the other way around. She wanted to run out of the cave and not stop until she was home, in her room, with the door closed.

"I guess that blows your theory," she said instead, recovering herself. Uncle Rupert must have gone someplace else. Tijuana, or something."

"Oh, sure," jeered Bran. "He drags the magic book all the way up to a cave and builds a big fire because he wants to go to Tijuana. You know as well as I do where he went. But for some reason, he didn't take the book."

Bran studied the softly glowing pages, as if the answer were locked in the intricate scrollwork.

"Hey, remember this?"

He had found the picture where Finn stood as a young boy in the middle of the sheltering wood. Fiona looked over her brother's shoulder at the intertwining green and golden branches from which every kind of bird and animal seemed to grow. Bran turned the pages, past strange pointed letters they couldn't read.

"Stop," said Fiona as Bran began turning faster. "Go back to that picture of the red deer in the woods."

"This one?"

"That's it. It gives me a funny feeling, kind of sad and lonesome." Fiona examined the delicate creature with the enormous eyes.

"It's just a deer," said Bran. "Help me get some sticks and build a fire, will you?"

Fiona gave the picture a last, longing look. "Why do you want to build a fire?"

"Because it's getting dark." Bran dropped a load of sticks at the mouth of the cave. "C'mon."

Fiona looked around. It *was* getting dark. "Let's take the book back to New York. I don't feel like spending the night in the house without Uncle Rupert."

"That's not what I had in mind." Bran left the cave.

"Just what did you have in mind?" huffed Fiona. "If you're not too busy to answer a question from a mere *older* sister?"

"I should have brought my hatchet," muttered Bran, standing over a fallen log. "Give me a hand, Fiona. We'll burn the whole thing."

Fiona wiped her hands on her jeans and watched Bran set fire to the pile of sticks and leaves and assorted logs they had dragged over. How had she let him talk her into building a fire?

Bran surveyed his work with pride, then went over to the magic book and opened it to the picture of the boy Finn in the woods.

"Would you mind telling me what's going on here?" asked Fiona.

"We've got the magic book, and the fire, and the cave, and it's Halloween, one of the four magic nights of the year when we can slip through time," said Bran. "So I thought we might as well try it."

"Gee, that's a fabulous idea, Bran. Too bad you don't know the Druid chant. Well, what can you do, huh? Let's go home." Fiona reached for the book.

Bran grabbed Fiona's wrist. "I do know it. I memorized it from last time."

All the hairs on Fiona's body stood on end. She was only too familiar with her brother's talent for memorization. If he said he knew the chant, he did.

"I'm going, Fiona, with you or without you. Uncle Rupert is there and he knows about our dad. I'm going to find him and find our dad, or find out who he is. If Uncle Rupert can't help me, Finn will."

Fiona stared at her brother.

"You could catch a fly with your mouth open like that," remarked Bran.

"Just what makes you think . . ." sputtered Fiona. "What makes you think that Uncle Rupert has anything to do with our dad?"

"I feel it."

"He feels it." Fiona addressed an imagined audience outside the cave. "No proof. He just feels it."

"No, really, Fiona," Bran persisted. "Remember that show on TV about dowsing for water, where they take a forked stick and wander around over the ground and, suddenly, wham! The stick points straight down! And that's where they dig their well. I feel the same way about this. Wham! I know I gotta go find Uncle Rupert because he will lead me to our dad."

Fiona looked at her little brother and suddenly realized she didn't know him at all anymore. When had he grown so big? He was almost as tall as she was, and much stronger. There used to be a time when she could drag him, kicking and screaming, wherever she wanted him to go. And since when had he become so smart? He had tricked her into coming up to the cave with him. He had planned it! She was used to tricking him. When had all this changed?

"You want to go? Go ahead," said Fiona, trying a little psychology. "Maybe I'll turn your room into a clubhouse for my friends while you're away. Ma will probably miss you a lot, so we'll have to go to the movies to take her mind off things, and eat in Chinese restaurants—"

Bran looked unconcerned. "You'd better go now, while there's still enough light to see your way down the path."

Fiona walked out of the cave. "How can you do this to Ma?" she challenged, one last time.

"I'm not leaving forever," argued Bran. "I'm just going to find out what Uncle Rupert knows about our dad, and then I'm coming back—probably." He muttered the last word under his breath but Fiona heard it only too clearly.

Fiona looked out at the darkening woods and back to her brother standing resolutely by the fire. He was determined to go. She could see that. Again she remembered how difficult it had been to persuade Bran to come home with her last time. What if he stayed this time?

Fiona pictured herself taking the bus to New York City alone. How could she tell Sadie she had let Bran go back two thousand years all by himself?

"He probably can't do it anyway," Fiona rationalized. "After all, he's only a kid." He never guessed

her card when he tried to do the Hocus-Pocus Splendif-
erous Card Trick.

"Count me in," said Fiona. "But if it doesn't work
after fifteen minutes, can we go home? This fire reminds me of toasted marshmallows, which reminds me
that we haven't had dinner."

"Don't mess me up with any of your wisecracks.
You have to concentrate for this to work," warned
Bran.

Bran assumed what he hoped was a Druid-looking
expression and began his chant: "Parthalon, Cessari,
Nemid—"

Fiona snickered.

"Fiona! Get out if you can't get serious."

"I can't help it. You look funny."

"Keep your eyes on the fire and concentrate, or it's
not going to work."

"It's not going to work anyway," thought Fiona,
when ten minutes later Bran was still chanting for all
he was worth and they hadn't moved even thirty sec-
onds back in time. She thought of all the hundreds of
years they had to move back through, and she knew a
nine-year-old boy couldn't possibly pull it off.

They must have put a green log on the fire. It was
beginning to smoke, making her dizzy. Animals rushed
by. Animals—or spirits. The very air was alive. The
wind rustled the pages of the book on the stone behind

them. Fiona turned around and saw that the book had blown open now to the page of the red deer. She watched as the deer grew larger and larger, coming off the page toward her. She tried to scream, but she had lost her voice.

"Bran," she wanted to cry, "now look what you've done. You've lost me!" But all that came out was a long, thin wail, stretching far back over centuries, searching for the rest of Fiona McCool.

5

"I did it! It worked! Wait till I tell Finn! Woo-ee!"
Fiona sat up and rubbed her eyes. Her brother was
turning cartwheels in the wet grass, whooping and
shouting and singing his own praises to the skies.

"You didn't think I could do it, did you? Huh?"
Bran crowed.

"Do what?" Fiona asked crossly.

"Get us to Ireland. But I did! I did! I'm a natural-born
Druid."

Fiona looked around. She was sitting on the grassy
bank of a broad river. The grass seemed to go on for
miles. Sheep and cattle browsed in the meadows.
Nearby, a field had been set aside for planting.

"What makes you think this is Ireland?"

"Because it smells like Ireland," said Bran confidently.

"It sure doesn't look like the Ireland I know," said Fiona. "We walked clear across Ireland with Finn and it was all trees. This looks like farms to me. We never saw farms in Ireland, or sheep either."

"What are you griping about? So we're not in exactly the same part as before. I got us here. That was the hardest part. Now we'll find Finn and Uncle Rupert. I can do anything." He scanned the unfamiliar countryside. "We might have to walk a little, that's all," he added. He was beginning to wish he had left his sister home.

"All right." Fiona stood up. "Let's go find someone and ask where we are. I just hope we don't come across any churls. Bring the book."

"I don't have it."

"What do you mean you don't have it?"

"I don't have it. It must not have come with us."

Fiona felt weak. "But then we can't go home again."

"Who cares about going home?" said Bran carelessly. "I'll be with Finn."

Fiona looked around wildly at the river, the green hills, and her little brother standing so sure before her. "Bran! You nincompoop!" she screamed, shaking him by the shoulders. "You idiot! We're lost, you little jerk. At least we used to have a mother and a home.

Now we've got nothing! We're nothing! Can't you understand that, you—bran brain, you?"

"Tut-tut, they were out prancing and dancing about and missed the cockcrow. Now they can't get back inside their hill," someone said.

Fiona jumped guiltily. A boy was standing behind them, a boy about thirteen or fourteen.

Fiona smiled back, dropping her hands to her sides.

"I was just strangling my brother," she explained.

The boy nodded. "Happens in the best of families, up here with us Christian folk, and down inside the hills of Ireland, where you Everlasting Ones abide. Some of the loveliest songs are written about people who strangle their brothers."

The boy was dressed in the ancient Irish way, in tunic and cape. His eyes were as blue as the river and his shoulder-length hair was black enough to be almost blue. His cheeks were so red that Fiona would have suspected him of wearing rouge, but somehow she knew better.

"We're not Everlasting Ones," explained Fiona. "I'm Fiona McCool and this is my brother Bran. We just slipped in from another time, and Bran and I were having an argument over where we landed."

"Ah! Mac Cools," said the boy. "O'Kelley's my name, not a magic name like yours, but a proud one. Legaire O'Kelley. Happy to meet you."

Fiona was about to ask why Legaire thought McCool was a magic name, when Bran butted in.

"And I'm happy to meet you," he said enthusiastically. "I was just going to have to punch my sister out to calm her down. She doesn't have much confidence in my Druid powers. She thought I messed up, but now that she knows she's in Ireland, she'll be O.K. You wouldn't happen to know a guy named Finn, would you? He's head of the Fianna."

"And what kind of a poet would I be if I didn't know one of Ireland's great heroes?" said Legaire. "And if I couldn't recite all the wondrous deeds of Finn and the Fianna—"

"No, I mean, could you tell us where he lives?" interrupted Bran.

"He lives in the hearts of his countrymen," Legaire went on merrily.

"No, no, we're trying to find him, don't you see?" Bran broke in again.

Legaire took a long look at Fiona and Bran. Fiona realized they must look pretty strange to him, in their dungarees and down jackets.

"I don't really understand," said Legaire slowly. "Finn is a legendary hero. He isn't someone you'd expect to meet as you go tripping down the road. There's a funny old monk up in Clonmacnoise who might know something about this. Maybe you'd better come along. I'm afraid your questions are too complicated for the likes of me!"

"Monk?" asked Fiona, growing more and more suspicious. "I don't remember any monks in Ireland. You wouldn't happen to know what year this is, would you, Legaire?"

Legaire grinned as if Fiona were teasing him. "Since we've been having the same year for some time, I think I'm pretty sure by now that it's 839 A.D."

"839 A.D.?" Bran was stunned. "But that's impossible. I said all the right words. The book was open to the right page—"

"But it turned," Fiona suddenly recalled. "The pages turned because of the wind, just as the chant started working."

"They did?"

"Yes, to the picture of the red deer, remember?"

"Oh, no!" wailed Bran. "Why didn't you tell me, you big dummy?"

"How could I tell you when my throat was already in a different time zone?" yelled Fiona. "You should have put a rock on the book. You were the big know-it-all Druid."

Bran opened his mouth to shout another insult at his sister, but he changed his mind. She was right. It was his own stupid fault. The page had turned. They were in 839 A.D. without the magic book, and he would never see Finn again. Bran threw himself, sobbing, on the ground.

Legaire knelt beside Bran. "Now see here," he advised. "This won't do at all." He glanced over his shoulder. "There's Culdees about, and if one should see you like this, he'd say you needed a week of cold baths and fasting, and I don't think, being as you're a Mac Cool, you'd take to it too well."

Bran lifted his face from the grass. "What's a Culdee?"

"Someone who's been chosen by God," explained Legaire. "They're wonderful, wonderful, and we need them, but they're kind of rigorous, don't you know? The best thing for you would be to come home with me, get a little breakfast, and talk to this old monk, the scribe, who's working with my brother Angus."

Breakfast sounded good to the McCools, and it seemed possible that this old monk of Legaire's might be able to help them. It was their only lead, so they went with Legaire along a path by the riverbank.

As they walked, Legaire played a light skipping tune on his pipe. For a moment, Fiona forgot her troubles and began prancing beside her new friend. Bran was still trying to figure out how he had gone so terribly wrong when something strange caught his eye.

"Hey, look. There's a guy standing in the river. He's shouting at us."

Legaire hid his pipe in his cloak. "Oh, dear. That's my cousin, Connor the Culdee. He's as God-fearing a person as you'd ever want to meet, but he's the last person you'd want to meet looking like you do. Well, there's no help for it now. I'll see what he wants. You might stand behind me, if you will, and be ready to run."

"Legaire, bring my cloak!" bellowed cousin Connor the Culdee from the river.

Legaire ran to pick up a ragged cloak from the river-bank and carried it down to the water's edge.

"Make the woman turn away!" cried Connor.

Fiona looked around for a woman, then realized he was calling *her* a woman.

"Culdees aren't generally too fond of ladies," Legaire explained to Fiona.

Fiona looked critically at the gaunt man in the water. "It's just as well. I don't think the ladies would be too crazy about him either."

She examined the hills behind her while Connor came out of the water and Legaire wrapped him in his cloak.

"Isn't it a little cold to go swimming? I mean, it is the first of November," remarked Fiona when Connor was dressed.

"He does it every morning, all year," explained Legaire, rubbing the trembling, blue-lipped Culdee with his cloak. "He sings the Psalms in the river. It brings him closer to God."

"By the looks of him, he should get close to a good fire," quipped Fiona.

The Culdee glared at Fiona, then averted his eyes. "What demons have you brought me, Legaire?" he muttered. "Be they demon or be they human, or human with demon within? Methinks they need humbling." With that, the cadaverous Culdee made a lunge at the McCools.

"Run!" shouted Legaire, blocking the Culdee.

"Run where?" thought Fiona, but she and Bran were already tearing down the path. While her legs and arms were pumping up and down like a wind-up toy, while her body was flying over the ground so fast that all her eyes could see was a blur, Fiona's mind was stuck on one question: Where on earth could they hide?

Suddenly, a great rock loomed out of the mist before her.

"Quick! Hide! Behind the rock!" gasped Fiona.

Not daring to look back, the McCools scrambled up over the rock and dropped down on the other side. The first thing they saw was a narrow opening. They squeezed through without hesitation and stood, panting, just inside.

"If you're coming in, come in. Don't stand in the doorway blocking the light," said a querulous voice.

"Bran," Fiona scolded, catching her breath. "This is no time for games."

"That wasn't me, honest. I thought it was you."

"I am twelve years old. Twelve-year-olds don't fool around like that."

"Well, if it wasn't you and it wasn't me—"

6

Fiona and Bran nervously edged their way out of the cave. The voice within cackled: "You don't dare go out or the Culdee will get you!"

Indeed, at that very moment, the McCools heard someone thrashing around outside, and a voice boomed, "Heathens! Come out and be humbled!"

The McCools ducked back in.

"That's the way," encouraged the voice within. "Come closer. I've a lovely fire here."

Now the McCools could see the flicker of a fire deeper in the cave. As they inched their way along, they saw a tiny figure bent over the flames.

"Closer, closer," invited the cave dweller. "Did you bring a nice egg for Old Biddy Gwynn?"

An ancient hag was sitting over a pitifully small fire. Her straight silver hair came down to her waist, framing a face that was as old and worn as the stone walls of the cave she was living in.

"Did you bring me an egg? A heel of bread?" she wheedled.

"No, I'm sorry." Fiona tried to cover her astonishment. "This is kind of an unexpected visit. Next time, maybe."

The hag nodded. "Next time will be all right. Come, kiss Biddy on the cheek. If you do, I'll give you disguises, and you can walk right by that Culdee."

Up close, Biddy looked even worse. Her chin was covered with whiskery warts. The McCools began backing toward the mouth of the cave.

"Heathen children!" someone roared outside.

The McCools scurried back to Biddy Gwynn.

"Kiss a crone or get caught by a Culdee!" she cried. "Take your choice!"

Fiona and Bran rolled their eyes at each other. They didn't know which was worse.

"Ladies first," Bran said to his sister.

"Youngest first," countered Fiona.

"How about at once?" suggested Biddy.

"Heathens!" thundered the voice outside.

The McCools pecked Biddy quickly on either cheek. As they kissed her, it seemed as if they were kissing the cool smooth cheeks of a young girl. They drew back in amazement. Biddy chuckled.

"That wasn't so bad, was it?" she crooned. "Now let me find you some disguises."

Biddy rummaged through a pile of rags in the corner of the cave. Every once in a while, she'd throw something out, examine it, and stuff it back in again. Fiona tried not to think about lice and fleas and various skin diseases she had heard about.

At last Biddy emerged with what looked like a pile of dirty drapes, which she presented to the McCools. Fiona and Bran shook them out and found that both of them had a tunic and a cape. They were like the clothes Legaire had been wearing, and similar to the ones they had worn on their adventure with Finn.

"I never thought I'd be glad to get into a dress again," said Bran gruffly, struggling into his tunic.

"Suppose you tell Old Biddy what brought you here," prompted the hag.

"It was my dumb brother's idea," said Fiona. "He started fooling around with a magic book. He said he was going to find Finn, and our Uncle Rupert, and our father, or at least learn something about him. But all we found was a weirdo Culdee, who wants to humble us, whatever that means." She wondered why she was rattling on like this to an old woman who wouldn't understand a word of what she was saying.

Biddy Gwynn studied them carefully with her silver eyes. "You look fairly intelligent," she said. "I expect you'll find what you're looking for, if you keep your mind on it. Give Biddy a kiss before you go."

Unable to think of a polite way to decline, the McCools were once more forced to peck the old woman on her cheeks. Again, they were surprised at how smooth her face felt. Biddy was still laughing when they left.

The McCools peered outside the cave. No Connor. They crept around the rock and then shrank back. A hooded figure, his back to them, was sitting on a log, merrily piping. Pulling their cloaks around their faces, Fiona and Bran walked past the figure and glanced back quickly. It was Legaire.

"I had given you up for gone," said Legaire after they had greeted each other joyfully. "Where did you find those clothes?"

"In that cave." Fiona pointed. "We were hiding inside with Old Biddy Gwynn while Connor was searching the bushes."

Legaire smiled knowingly. "Ah, you Mac Cools like your stories," he said. "That's an old one, about the fairest maid in Ireland, the lovely Gwynn—"

"No, that wasn't this Gwynn," interrupted Fiona. "And it isn't some made-up story."

"Let him finish, will you?" asked Bran.

"The lovely Gwynn," continued Legaire, "who was changed by a jealous witch into a dragonfly for two hundred years."

"A dragonfly?"

"A beautiful dragonfly," Legaire went on. "But she didn't waste those two hundred years just flitting about. She went and studied with Cathbad the Druid, and when the spell was over, she was as powerful a Druid as old Cathbad had ever been, in a different way, of course."

"That wasn't our Biddy Gwynn," said Fiona. "Because if this Gwynn was a Druid, she would have done something about her looks, at least gotten rid of her warts."

"That's the funny thing about the Druid Gwynn," said Legaire. "When she became a Druid, she was as ugly as she had once been beautiful. When people asked her why, she said it was too dangerous being beautiful."

"Maybe this is the one!" cried Bran. "She sure is homely."

"Oh, no," said Legaire. "That was hundreds of years ago, before St. Patrick made Christians out of us. There are no Druids left now."

"Are you sure about that?" asked Bran. "Come on back to the cave. I'll show you the ugliest old lady you ever saw, and she calls herself Biddy Gwynn."

Legaire laughed, putting an arm around each of them. "You Mac Cools and your jokes," he said. "Wouldn't you rather come up for some nice hot stirabout and leave the cave for another day?"

Bran was about to object, but he remembered that he would probably have to kiss Biddy Gwynn if he went back to see her. Then, too, he was getting very hungry. "Where are we going for this stirabout?" he asked.

"Clonmacnoise."

"Is it far, this Clonmac—whatever place?" asked Fiona, who was feeling a little woozy after all the excitement on an empty stomach.

"You're walking right toward the city wall," said Legaire.

Now that Legaire had mentioned it, Fiona could see what looked like a man-made embankment, but she would hardly flatter it by calling it a wall. It was all overgrown with grass and shrubs. Some sure-footed sheep were grazing near the top. A stream ran at its base. "If he calls that a wall, he probably calls the stream a moat," Fiona said to herself.

Up close, Bran was not impressed with the fortifications around Clonmacnoise either. He was sure he could run right up them in a minute. The bridge across the stream was unimpressive as well. It was built of logs split in half lengthwise and laid side by side. If there were a battle, the logs would have to be pulled up and piled in front of the entrance, which would waste a lot of time. "They should at least put in a drawbridge," thought Bran.

A boy and his pigs ran by on the bridge, nearly knocking Fiona into the water. Legaire grabbed her arm.

"Now don't tell me you want to stand in the moat singing the Psalms," he joked.

"I think I'll wait until after breakfast anyway," remarked Fiona.

Fiona was glad Legaire was still holding her arm, for Clonmacnoise was so busy that it was dizzying at first. The quiet countryside had not prepared her for the hubbub of life within the walls. Pigs and chickens, dogs and cats, and children of every size ran freely among the jumble of round thatch-roofed huts. There didn't seem to be any plan to the way the houses were placed, except that the doors all faced the same direction. These doors were wide open as the inhabitants went about their morning housekeeping, tossing out bones and shells and other garbage to be trampled into the mud.

Fiona tried breathing through her mouth. "Is this a city?"

"This is the city of Clonmacnoise, and on top of the hill is the monastery," said Legaire.

"Are you a monk?" asked Fiona. She hoped not. He didn't look like one.

"I missed that divine calling," said Legaire, trying to sound regretful. "I've been away, studying to be a poet.

I came home because, as an O'Kelley, I am sworn to defend Clonmacnoise to the death."

Fiona looked around uneasily. She wondered what would threaten this confusion of huts and people. A girl about Fiona's age lugged a large baby across their path. Fiona suddenly remembered how utterly lost she and Bran were. She swallowed hard to keep from crying.

"Where's the monastery?" she asked, just to hear Legaire's voice again.

"Through this gate," said Legaire.

"Neat!" cried Bran. "It's a city inside a city."

The monastery of Clonmacnoise was surrounded by its own stone wall, separating it from the main city. Bran noted that this wall was carefully made, and although it was lower than the main one, it couldn't be climbed as easily. The stout oak gates would seal the entrance in case of attack.

The first thing the McCools saw as they passed through was a great stone cross about seven-feet high. Others of wood and stone pierced the sky. Except for the crosses, the monastery looked much the same as the town below.

Men and boys passed them on various errands.

"Can they be monks?" Fiona asked herself. They didn't look at all like the sweet potbellied statuettes of monks she sometimes saw in Woolworths. These were rough, gaunt men, with long flowing hair and daggers in their belts. Fiona kept a nervous eye out for Culdees, although she didn't know if she could tell a Culdee from a regular monk. Maybe *all* of them were Culdees! She hid her face in her hood.

"Let's look for brother Angus first," suggested Legaire.

The McCools followed Legaire, squeezing between two huts and soon finding themselves facing a sloping lawn. On the other side, a tiny steep-roofed building made of wood stood all by itself. Legaire called it a church, although it looked too small for a church, and it didn't have a steeple. As they went closer, the McCools could see the mournful faces carved on the lintel beam. Fiona could barely go through the narrow doorway without bumping her head.

It was snug but airy inside. Two bowls filled with burning oil hung from the rafters, and beneath each of these lamps was a monk bent in deep concentration over an easel. The younger monk looked like Legaire but was not as handsome, in Fiona's opinion. She assumed he was Legaire's brother Angus. The other monk looked exactly like—Uncle Rupert!

7

"Uncle Rupert!" cried the McCools.

"Oh, thank goodness. What a relief! When can we go home?" Fiona exclaimed.

Uncle Rupert frowned at the three children before him. "Legaire, I asked you not to bring any more of your hooligan friends in here. Angus and I must have quiet."

"It's Fiona and Bran, Uncle Rupert." Fiona threw back her hood. "Remember?"

Uncle Rupert blinked at them through his glasses. "Umph? Ah! So it is. Fiona and Bran. My, my. What are you doing here?"

"I was hoping you'd know," said Fiona.

"I know what *I* am doing here," said Uncle Rupert. "My friend Angus and I are working on a marvelous old legend, a survivor of pre-Christian times that has never been put in writing before. Think of it! Recited over lonely campfires, sung in great banquet halls, but never written, never read. What a mission for someone in his twilight years!"

Fiona peered over Uncle Rupert's shoulder. He had been painting letters in black, red, and gold on a sheet of parchment. There was something familiar about those queer pointy letters, but Fiona couldn't say what it was.

"It's nice *you're* so happy," said Bran grudgingly, "but I don't know what *we're* doing here. We wanted to be with Finn, and instead we landed in this fleabag monastery."

There was an uncomfortable silence. "He's young," Uncle Rupert apologized to Angus and Legaire. "And his education has been sadly lacking. He has no idea that Clonmacnoise is a great center of art and scholarship. To him it's a collection of mud huts. However, you are here, Bran, my boy," he said. "So you must be here for a reason. Look around Clonmacnoise. Visit the metalworkers, the stonecutters. Sit in on a Latin class. Your purpose here, your mission, will come to you in a few days, just as mine came to me."

Bran thought for a moment. Uncle Rupert had caught his imagination, suggesting that he had a mission in Clonmacnoise. "I was looking for my dad when

I started out," he said slowly. "Yeah, that will be my mission, finding my dad."

"You think you'll find your father here in Clonmacnoise?" asked Uncle Rupert. "What an intriguing idea. Whatever makes you think that?"

"You," said Bran. "You can help me. You were Ma's guardian. You must know who he was."

"Haven't the foggiest notion," said Uncle Rupert blandly. "Now if you'll excuse me, Angus and I are right in the middle—"

"But, Uncle Rupert," objected Bran. "You gotta know something. You were there."

"No, I wasn't. When your mother disappeared, I was teaching in Trinity College in Dublin, as I do every summer."

"Disappeared!"

Angus looked up from his work and nodded sympathetically. "It still happens here in Christian Ireland," he joined in. "Not too often, but now and again one of the Everlasting Ones takes a fancy to a young woman and throws up a Druid mist around her. Poof! Off she goes, into thin air!"

"Well, it had never happened before in Perry, New York. You can imagine the disturbance—reporters and policemen around the house for days," Uncle Rupert said, shaking his head, as if the reporters and policemen had upset him more than the disappearance of his niece. He dipped his quill into a small inkwell made from the tip of a cow's horn and carefully drew a letter on the parchment before him.

"When did she come back?" prompted Bran.

Uncle Rupert looked up at Bran as if he had forgotten he was there. "She came back with me, naturally, after I signed her out of the hospital." Again he returned to his work.

"What hospital?" shouted the McCools.

Uncle Rupert jumped, spoiling the letter he was working on. "I'm not deaf, you know," he said crossly. "Nearsighted, yes. Lame, yes. But not deaf—yet."

"This is very important to us," insisted Bran. "We never heard this story before."

"Very well." Uncle Rupert reluctantly put his brush up. "I was teaching at Trinity, about four years after your mother disappeared, when I received a telephone call from the hospital. Your mother had been found by a guard in the National Museum in Dublin. She was sitting in an ancient dugout canoe, twelve feet off the ground, with two howling babies in her arms. You can imagine the consternation she caused. She and the babies, and even the canoe, were dripping wet—"

"The Everlasting Ones are notorious for that kind of abandonment," broke in Angus. "Poor little thing has two children and she gets sent back." He shook his head. "Thank God we're a Christian country and don't believe in them anymore."

"But that's crazy!" exclaimed Fiona.

"I'll admit I was a little concerned for your mother's mental stability," Uncle Rupert agreed, "but she went back with me, found work as an actress in New York, and has been doing splendidly ever since. I never asked where the babies came from. Didn't think it was tactful . . ." he trailed off.

"What do you say now, Fioney Baloney? I was pretty smart, wasn't I, coming here to find Uncle Rupert?" bragged Bran, forgetting that he was only there by mistake.

Fiona didn't bother answering Bran's ridiculous boast. She was extremely alarmed by all Uncle Rupert had told them. It seemed as if her mother had been caught up in some ancient Irish magic. And in the center of this mysterious story was the question of who their father was. The Everlasting Ones were the gods of ancient Ireland. Could one of them have been their father? Fiona thought of the tales Finn had told them about the Everlasting Ones. All of them had strange habits. One could breathe fire, and another was extremely fat and could eat whole herds of cattle for dinner—not exactly her ideal dad.

Bran was more interested in the canoe. He questioned Uncle Rupert about the exact dimensions of the craft.

"Go down to the river and look," said Uncle Rupert. "It was a typical dugout canoe. You'll find fifty down there if you find one."

That was all Bran had to hear. In a flash, he and Legaire were out the door. Fiona went running after them.

"Why do you want to see canoes?" asked Fiona, catching up with the boys as they crossed the bridge over the moat.

"The trouble with you," said Bran, "is you don't know how to trust your instincts, if you have any. Now, I've got great instincts. As soon as Uncle Rupert said 'canoe,' my instincts told me to go find one."

"I think what you're calling instinct is just the first thing that comes into your head," grumbled Fiona.

The boats in the little harbor near Clonmacnoise weren't very elaborate. Some were canoes, made of huge hollowed-out logs. Others were made like baskets, with hides stretched over the outside. One of the dugout canoes was lying upside down on the riverbank.

"This must be the same kind they found Ma in," said Bran.

"Why don't you put your hands on it and see if you get a vision?" Fiona was being sarcastic. To her embarrassment, he did just that.

"It's no use," said Bran after a while. "I don't feel anything."

"I don't know if I can take this Great Swami stuff much longer," muttered Fiona. "Let's go back up. We never did get our breakfast."

Fiona broke away from the boys and began climbing

the hill toward the city. Suddenly she stopped and squatted down on the ground.

"What's the matter?" asked Bran. "Can't go another step without a Pop-Tart?"

"Deer tracks." Fiona was frowning at some marks in the mud.

"Yeah, so what? There are deer in Ireland, too," said Bran. "Red ones, remember?"

"Red deer," said Fiona, as if in a trance. She looked up at Bran and Legaire staring down at her. "Uh, I've had a thing about deer lately," she said, getting to her feet. "Nevermind. Let's get some food."

Legaire took the McCools over to the cookshed, a three-sided shelter with no roof. The cook was a monk whom Legaire had known since he was small. He was happy to ladle out three big portions of what he called stirabout, and what the McCools called oatmeal. With a wink, he put a big dab of honey in the middle of each serving. Legaire sat on a bench, with a McCool on either side of him.

As Bran ate, he thought about what the next stage in his plan should be. Right now, his instincts were telling him nothing. He wouldn't admit it to Fiona, but he was stumped. Uncle Rupert's clue had seemed so great at first, but it had led to a dead end. He wished his magic had been strong enough to take him back to Finn. Finn would know how to help him.

It was beginning to rain. Bran retreated into his cloak. Somehow it was worse wearing these clothes, being in Ireland, being close to Finn but so impossibly far away. He felt his eyelids growing heavy. Maybe he could find a dry patch of straw and take a nap.

Fiona ate her oatmeal, trying not to think about her mother. The harder she tried not to, the clearer she saw her, looking not as she did on stage, looking not like the delivery boy, or even the visiting countess. Fiona saw her with her red hair pulled smoothly away from her face, with her eyes enormous and sad. So sad. Fiona choked on a lump in her oatmeal.

Legaire thumped her on the back.

"Thanks," coughed Fiona.

"The woodcock sounds in the bracken budding—" recited Legaire.

"The red stag bells in the swamp," finished Fiona.

"Then you've studied with the poets."

"A little," admitted Fiona. She had responded automatically, but now she remembered that Irish poets often played a game with each other. One would make up a line of poetry and the other would have to finish it.

"I thought you, with your nimble tongue, might be a poet," said Legaire. "But where is your harp?"

"I don't play—"

"Every poet should play the harp," he reproached her. "I could give you lessons if you like."

For a moment, Fiona was inexplicably flustered. "I do like," she stumbled.

Legaire took her hand. "Come back to the church with me. I left my harp there."

"Where are you going?" asked Bran, rousing himself from his stupor.

"I'm going to teach your sister how to play the harp."

"Teach me, too."

"By all means," said Legaire. "Come along."

Fiona began to wonder why she'd even brought Bran with her in the first place.

8

It was cozy inside the church, with the rain hitting the wooden roof. "Like being under a boat," thought Fiona. "Like being under that dugout canoe down by the river." Fiona hadn't told Bran, but she *had* felt something then, as if there were a memory connected with a canoe. But it wasn't a memory Fiona wanted to call up.

To take her mind off things, Fiona watched Legaire. After showing the McCools some basic chords on the harp, he played them a song. Fiona was sure she would never learn to play like Legaire. He made it seem so easy, as if the harp already knew the tune and he only had to touch it to coax the music out.

Fiona stood up and, drawing her cloak around her, went over to Angus's easel to see what he was laboring over with such concentration. It was a picture that filled the entire sheet of parchment, a picture so intricate that it had probably taken weeks to do. Today he was putting on the finishing touches—a streak of gold to highlight a vine or a leaf, a few gold flecks in the eyes, the great sad eyes.

"The deer," whispered Fiona. There, staring out at her, was the same little red deer that had disturbed her so in Uncle Rupert's magic book.

"Uncle Rupert. Did you see this? What Angus is drawing? It looks just like a page from—your magic book!"

"What book?"

"Your magic book, the one you had in Perry, New York. The one we used to come here. You remember."

"There is so much I have forgotten about that time," sighed Uncle Rupert. ". . . strange, gray areas."

"Bran," Fiona appealed to her brother. "Come see this picture. Isn't this the same one that's in Uncle Rupert's magic book?"

Bran sauntered over and gave it a quick glance. "Never saw it before in my life."

"Bull!" cried Fiona. "It's right out of the magic book!" But as she examined the picture, she wasn't so sure. The colors were so much brighter than she remembered.

"Fiona," said Uncle Rupert, who was losing patience

with all the chattering around him. "I have a great sense of urgency about this manuscript. These are perilous times, times of great upheaval, and I must get the work completed as soon as possible. If you can't be quiet, I'll have to ask you to leave."

"But the magic book," protested Fiona. "How could you forget?"

"My dear, when will you ever learn that silence is golden?" intoned her uncle.

Bran smirked at her from over Uncle Rupert's shoulder.

That was the limit. "You're crazy!" cried Fiona. "You and Bran. Sitting around in a shack in the rain—you writing some nutty fairy tale, and Bran looking for his father. Who cares about him? What kind of a father could he be if he left Ma in an old canoe with no alimony or child support? You're both bananas, and you deserve each other!"

Fiona stormed out of the church and right into the arms of Connor the Culdee.

They each jumped back in horror.

"A woman!" cried Connor, as if he had seen a toad. "In the church! It's the heathen woman! Fie!"

Fiona didn't wait around to hear what other opinions Connor had of her. She ran. If she could have run home and left Bran and Uncle Rupert behind, she would have. But she only ran as far as a corner of the monastery, where there was a covered well in the middle of an orchard. Fiona, feeling wet and extremely sorry for herself, took shelter at the side of the well.

Connor hadn't followed her. At least that was something. "What a creep," she said to herself, flicking a pebble off into the water.

A dark shape rose to investigate the splash. A fish. Was it sanitary, Fiona wondered, to have a fish in a well? She hoped this wasn't where her drinking water had been coming from. Fiona leaned over to get a better look. Now she saw two fat fish swimming around.

"Having a chat with the sacred trout, I see."

Fiona nearly fell in, but a strong arm caught her just in time. She turned around to find herself face to face with Legaire.

"Oh! You scared me. You really shouldn't come up behind someone who's leaning over a well," she scolded.

"I'm sorry." Legaire let go of her. "I heard Cousin Connor denouncing you and came to see if you needed help. Don't take it to heart. Connor denounces all of us, regularly. That's the purpose of Culdees."

"Why do you call them sacred trout?" Bran popped up on the other side of Legaire.

Once again Fiona had to ask herself why Bran had to be everywhere she was.

"Every monastery has its sacred fish," explained Legaire. "They protect us from our enemies."

"Enemies?" Bran's eyes lit up. "Who are your enemies?"

"Until now, the monks of Durrow—"

"Monks fighting monks?" It didn't sound right to Fiona.

"The monks of Clonmacnoise and Durrow have been fighting for two hundred years," said Legaire. "There's a whole song about it. Want me to sing it?"

"Yeah!" said Bran. He was beginning to like Clonmacnoise more and more.

Legaire sang them a long song, with many verses, about how the monks of Durrow had made a cattle raid on Clonmacnoise and how the young son of their protector, Dermod Duff, was killed. The verses went on describing how the monks of Durrow tried to take revenge on the sons of Kelley.

"It sounds risky, being a son of Kelley," said Bran when the song was over. "Are there any of them still alive?"

"I am a son of that Kelley," said Legaire proudly. "It's an honor I share with Angus and Cousin Connor."

"No kidding!" Bran was impressed. "Did they ever try to, you know, take revenge on you?"

"They did," said Legaire, strumming lightly on his harp. "Many times. But the first time was the most frightening. I've been thinking of making up a new verse about it. When we were very small, the monks of Durrow came storming right over the monastery wall. I remember my mother led the three of us out through a secret tunnel. We just barely escaped."

"That must have been a traumatic experience," said Fiona sympathetically.

"No, it was an underground passage," said Legaire. "It was very old, from before the monastery was built."

Bran laughed. Fiona gave up.

"But there's much worse than the monks of Durrow threatening us now," said Legaire, looking around as if he expected this new enemy to come crawling over the wall.

The McCools looked, too. "Who? Who are they?" whispered Bran, as if they might be within earshot.

"I call them the Outsiders," said Legaire. "I was in Armagh when they swooped down in their long boats with the tall bright sails. They laid that great monastery to waste and ruin. Especially the books." Legaire shook his head. "Those heathen cowards hate our books."

"Why cowards?" asked Bran. "They're not afraid to fight, are they?"

"Cowards because they wear helmets and vests to protect them in battle," Legaire said. "We scorn such protection."

"Yeah, well, you have the sacred trout," joked Fiona. Bran mentally pushed her into the well.

"We'll need more than sacred trout when the Outsiders come," said Legaire. "We'll need trained fighting men and weapons. I came to warn my kinsmen about the Outsiders, but they prefer to worry about the monks of Durrow."

"What you need is a demonstration," said Bran enthusiastically. "We'll get a bunch of guys out in front of the church fighting with swords, and people will come by and ask what we're doing, and we'll say we're getting ready for the Outsiders."

"That's brilliant!" said Legaire. "I have some swords. Want to start now?"

"Why not?" cried Bran. "There's no time to lose!"

Fiona watched the boys race back to the church. She didn't like the sound of this enemy, the Outsiders, and she didn't like the way Bran was getting carried away with the idea of defending Clonmacnoise.

9

That night, Fiona slept in a thatched hut with Uncle Rupert, Bran, Legaire, and Angus. Or rather, Fiona lay in the far corner of the hut listening to Uncle Rupert and Angus snoring. Uncle Rupert's snore was low and rumbling. Angus's was higher, with some whistling thrown in. When she wasn't listening to the snoring, Fiona was worrying about Connor the Culdee or the Outsiders bursting into the hut. When she wasn't worrying about that, she was worrying about Sadie. She felt terrible that she had lied to her mother. It had seemed like such an innocent little thing, and now who knew when, and if, she would ever see Sadie again so she could explain.

Finally, just as a pale light penetrated the hut, Fiona fell asleep. When she awoke, everyone was gone.

She stuck her head cautiously out the door. No Culdees. No Outsiders. Pulling her hood close around her face, Fiona started up the hill for the church. With her back hunched against the stiff wind blowing from the river and her head down to avoid being spotted by Culdees, Fiona couldn't miss the sight of sharp fresh deer tracks close to the hut.

"A deer? Inside the monastery?" wondered Fiona. As she said this, she realized that she had been dreaming of deer, of a certain red deer.

"Fiona! Over here!" It was Legaire. He, Bran, Angus, and even Uncle Rupert were assembled on the green in front of the church, swords in their hands. Legaire and Bran were fencing. Uncle Rupert was stiffly poking his weapon around Angus, who was trying not to laugh.

"We're practicing for when the Outsiders come," said Legaire.

"I've decided that's my mission!" cried Bran, jumping up and down in his excitement. "That's why I came— to defend Clonmacnoise against the Outsiders!" He lunged toward Fiona.

"Terrific." Fiona waved away the sword Legaire was offering her. "No, thanks. I have something I want to do in the church."

The finished picture of the red deer was still on the easel. Fiona forced herself to take a good hard look. She examined the dainty hooves, the slender legs, the rounded body, those sad eyes. Whether or not it was the same picture that she had seen in Uncle Rupert's magic book, she couldn't tell, but it had a similar effect on her. Her breath was coming in short gasps.

She stumbled out of the church.

Uncle Rupert had abandoned his fencing practice and was limping toward her. "You're looking green," he observed.

Fiona took a deep breath. "I'm all right." She tried changing the subject. "What about you? I don't think this Irish weather is too great for your arthritis."

Her uncle lowered himself stiffly onto a stump. "I have to spend more time in the sweat house, that's all."

Fiona stood beside him, watching the others at their practice. "What's the story of the red deer?" she asked at last.

Uncle Rupert regarded her uncertainly. "Oh, you mean the doe. The one Angus was working on. No one knows. We only know there should be a doe in the legend somewhere, and Angus was inspired to draw it, so we'll include it, even without the story."

"You mean it's a lost legend? Doesn't anyone remember?"

Uncle Rupert shook his head. "Believe me, we've asked every resident and passing poet. It was forgotten somewhere in the telling and retelling."

"What about someone who's lived a real long time,

who maybe heard it as a kid? Are there any old people here?"

"I must say, it never occurred to us to ask some of our more venerable brethren," said Uncle Rupert. "Although I don't think too many of them are interested in pre-Christian myths."

Fiona thought of Biddy Gwynn. Maybe she remembered the story; she'd certainly been around long enough. "She's probably senile," Fiona told herself.

She watched her brother fencing with Legaire. In one day he had switched his mission from finding his father to defending Clonmacnoise.

She hadn't forgotten her mission to get them all home safely again. But she didn't seem any closer to her goal. She'd be even farther away if Bran fell into a fight with the dreaded Outsiders. Fiona shivered inside her cape. What she should do is find him a good clue and get him back on the track of looking for his father. At least that would take his mind off fighting and keep him safe until she could figure out a way home.

She started walking toward the church. Bran had said her trouble was that she didn't follow her instincts. Well, she had an instinct, a strong one, about that red doe.

"It's not fair," she thought, hiding Angus's painting under her cloak and stealing out of the church. "After all, it was Bran's idea to go looking for our father. I was perfectly happy at home worrying about book reports."

By the time Fiona reached the bridge over the moat, a cold wet wind was whipping up the river and sending needles of rain into her face. For a moment, Fiona thought she must be crazy, going out in the rain to see an ancient woman who lived in a rock to ask her if she knew a story about a deer. But crazy as it was, Fiona realized it was the only thing she could think of to do.

There were fresh deer tracks on the riverbank. Fiona held the parchment closer and hurried on.

Had she made a mistake? The rock beside the river looked grim and deserted. With her heart beating a little too fast, Fiona pushed herself through the narrow crack and called into the dark, "Biddy Gwynn?"

There was a long moment when Fiona considered running away. Then a dry voice croaked, "Come in."

Fiona saw a pale fire in the darkness, and close to the fire, a glint of silver, the silver hair of Biddy Gwynn. Cautiously, Fiona approached the old woman, who was sitting with stonelike stillness, her eyes closed. Fiona cleared her throat.

"I'd rather be greeted with a kiss," said the crone with alarming coyness.

"I—ah—brought you three eggs," said Fiona. "That's

all I could find. Someone must have collected them before me." Fiona laid the eggs at her feet.

"That's nice," said Biddy, "but you still have to give me a kiss." She turned a warty cheek.

"Oh well, I've come this far," said Fiona to herself. She gingerly kissed Biddy's cheek and was once more startled at how smooth and young the skin felt. Again, Biddy cackled at Fiona's surprise.

The silver eyes studied Fiona for a minute or two.

"You didn't come all this way to give an old hag some eggs, did you?" Biddy prompted Fiona, who was tongue-tied for once.

"No," said Fiona finally, wondering for a moment why she *had* come. "I came because I thought you might be able to help me find out who my father was."

Old Biddy Gwynn said nothing.

"I don't even care a whole lot," Fiona went on, "or maybe I'm afraid, but my nutty brother, Bran. . . . You met him, remember—" Still no sign from Biddy Gwynn. Fiona wondered why she was bothering with this old woman, who was probably deaf as well as senile. "Anyway, Bran brought us here looking for our father but now he's forgotten and all he wants to do is fight the Outsiders. So I thought if I came up with a good clue, I'd get him interested in finding out about his father again and he'd forget about fighting and I could keep him safe until I figure out a way to get us home." Fiona finished, breathless.

A log popped in Biddy's fire. She didn't move. Fiona wondered if she were dead, when Biddy stretched her clawlike fingers toward the parchment which was clutched, forgotten, in Fiona's hand.

"Oh!" Fiona jumped. "This picture gives me a funny feeling," she explained, handing it over. "I thought maybe you would know the story that goes with it. It's a lost story no one can remember."

Old Biddy Gwynn held the picture up close to her face, then very far away. She turned it so the light from the fire fell upon it, then she sighed. She clucked her tongue, and even sang a few snatches of song under her breath.

"Oh, brother," thought Fiona. "What a waste of time. The old girl's lost her marbles."

"Could you just," Fiona pleaded, "remember one thing about the story that you could tell me—"

Old Biddy's eyes snapped at Fiona. "I remember the whole thing, vividly."

"You do! Would you tell it to me, please? I don't know why, but I think the story might help me 'n' Bran find out who our father was."

Biddy smiled. "I imagine you might have quite an interest in the story of this red doe, being as you are a Mac Cool. And I could tell you about the red doe, which might help you slightly on your way. Or," and Biddy Gwynn drew herself up on her seat, "I could *send* you into the story." She poked at the fire and her eyes glowed with the embers. "Yes, send you into the story with your brother. That would be a nice piece of work for an old Druid. Don't get to practice much anymore.

"Bring the boy and the picture to the Druid grove at sunset. And bring me a jug full of Clonmacnoise mead." She smacked her lips. "That will be my payment."

Fiona rolled up the parchment and put it back inside her cloak. So the old lady wanted to draw things out. Well, it would be a good idea if Bran heard what she had to say, too. He might have some more of his famous instincts about what she was going to tell them.

"How do I find the Druid grove?" asked Fiona, after she had obediently kissed Biddy once more on the cheek.

Old Biddy Gwynn laughed. "That will be the easiest part," she said, dismissing Fiona with a wave of her hand.

In spite of the rain and the cold, Legaire and Bran were still at their fencing practice when Fiona returned. The lawn outside the church was torn and muddy from their struggles.

"Too bad Finn isn't here with us," Bran was bragging to Legaire. "He could jump six feet in the air! I saw him do it! And he wasn't afraid of anything—"

"No churl was too tall—" Legaire joined in.

"Even a fire-breathing monster—" Bran cried.

Fiona stood listening until the boys noticed her. "I'm glad you're having a good time, Bran," she said. "But if you'll recall, the reason you brought us here in the first place was to find out who our father was. While you have been fooling around with swords, I have been following my instincts. I went to see Old Biddy Gwynn all by myself," she said proudly, "to ask her if she knew the story of the red doe. And Biddy Gwynn said that the red doe might be a very interesting story for McCools who are looking for their father. But she wanted you to hear it, too, so I said we'd both meet her at the Druid grove. Do you know where the Druid grove is, Legaire?"

Bran frowned at his sister. It was true that he had temporarily given up on finding his father, but why would he want to go listen to an old lady tell a story about a deer? What good would that do?

Fiona was flattered to see that her words had made a much greater impression on Legaire.

"Old Biddy Gwynn! Have you really seen her then? Why not? You *are* Mac Cools, after all. If anyone could see Biddy Gwynn, it would be a Mac Cool. And she wants to meet you at the Druid grove. I would dearly love to take you there myself. When did she say?"

"Sundown."

Legaire smiled. "A properly magic time of day. And it so happens that everyone will be at Vespers then."

10

All day the sun had been sulking behind a heavy curtain of clouds, but now the clouds were getting tattered around the edges, and the sun was able to peek through for just a few moments before it had to leave for the other side of the world. It had time to see four monks on the green, clanging cowbells. It watched as men from every corner of Clonmacnoise hurried to assemble in front of the church. Just as the sun passed over the horizon, it saw the entire company sink to its knees, sending a hymn up into the air.

The sun left too soon to see three figures slip past the singing monks.

"Why all this hush-hush stuff?" asked Bran, who was enjoying himself immensely but couldn't figure out why they had to be so secretive about the whole thing.

"The Druid grove," whispered Legaire, as he led them quickly over a bog behind the monastery, "is full of the old magic. The monks have tried to cut it down many times, but something always prevents them, so they've said that no one is to enter it. And no one does, unless he has his mind set on doing some magic."

Fiona shifted the jug of mead to her other arm. "What kind of magic do you think she's going to do? I thought she was going to tell us a story."

"I don't know," said Legaire eagerly. "That's what I want to see."

After a while, Legaire stopped and pointed to a small hill crowned by twisted oaks, silhouetted in the twilight. "There it is."

"It's kind of spooky looking," Fiona whispered nervously.

"Dee-mons! Woe betide he who enters the cursed grove!" came a wail floating on the breeze.

The McCools jumped. "Maybe we better not go in," said Fiona.

"On the contrary, I think you'd better run for it," suggested Legaire. "That voice was from behind. Look."

The McCools turned to see Connor the Culdee striding over the bog, brandishing a big wooden cross.

"Flee toward the grove," advised Legaire. "I'll do my best to divert my dear cousin and join you later."

"Connor, my darling!" he called out to the Culdee.

"So glad you came along. You're absolutely right, you know. That's what I was telling these travelers. 'Go ye not into the cursed grove,' or words to that effect. I'm certainly not going. But let them do as they like. They're more than half-heathen anyway. Let's go home and sing the Psalms, shall we? But let's not sing them in the river. Let's do them genuflecting. Fifty times for each Psalm. It would do me good, don't you think?"

The McCools raced for the grove. Just as they reached the hill, they looked back and saw Legaire walking a reluctant Connor back toward Clonmacnoise.

Fiona was feeling less and less enthusiastic about her meeting with Biddy Gwynn, but if she turned back, she might run into Connor. Still, this grove gave her a very uncomfortable feeling, as if someone were watching her. She looked around and found herself staring at a jackdaw, perched on a low branch, following her progress with yellow eyes. Then she saw another jackdaw, and another. They all seemed to be looking at her. Fiona was going to ask Bran if he ever remembered being stared at by the birds at home, when a sudden crackling of underbrush made her grab his arm. A deer bounded out from the trees, circled up to the top of the hill, and disappeared over the other side.

Bran whistled. "I gotta admit you're on to something. I thought you were just messing around, but you're on to something. I can smell it."

Bran's praise encouraged Fiona. "Look," she pointed to the crown of the grove. "There's Old Biddy Gwynn."

The tiny Druid was standing among the oaks. Behind her hung a silver crescent moon. She watched the McCools approach and reached out for the jug. Fiona gave it to her. Biddy pried out the cork and put the honey liquor to her lips.

"Ah! Those bell-clangers know how to make mead, I'll say that for them." She leaned against a nearby oak. "Build a big fire. Big! Right here! Then we'll get down to business." She tipped back her head and took another drink.

"Hurry up," Fiona told Bran as they gathered up all the dry wood they could find. "Before she gets too tight to talk."

"Yes! Yes! That's it! A high fire, one that those meddle-some monks will be able to see all the way from Clonmacnoise!" Biddy Gwynn cheered as the fire threw wild shadows on the trees.

"Don't you think you'd better tell us the story before the monks decide to come and investigate?" asked Fiona, thinking of one Culdee in particular.

"I'm not going to *tell* you the story," said Biddy, her eyes gleaming from the fire, or the mead. "I'm going to *send* you *into* the story. Feel the ancient magic moving through the treetops." She leaned her silver head back and laughed.

The McCools could see the trees swaying, as if at Biddy Gwynn's command.

"Feel the ancient magic rising up from beneath your feet," crooned the Druid.

"Yes!" cried Bran. "I feel it! I feel it!"

"Now give me the picture of the red doe," whispered Biddy Gwynn.

Fiona unrolled the parchment and laid it out on a fallen log for Biddy.

Biddy squatted down beside the log with an agility that didn't go with her age. "Come down close," she invited.

The McCools knelt beside her.

"I am going to send you through my mind into the story of the red doe. I am going to let you *see*. The story takes four years, but you will fly through, touching upon it here and there."

"Would you mind explaining a little more?" asked Fiona, who was beginning to think she had bought more with her jug of mead than she had bargained for. "I mean, just how are you going to *send* us into a story?"

"The ravens." Biddy pointed a gnarled finger at two small ravens, nearly hidden in the vines that twisted to form the frame of the picture.

"How come I never noticed them before?" wondered Fiona.

"You will be the ravens," continued Biddy. "You will see the story of the red doe from the eyes of the ravens."

"Neat-o!" cried Bran.

"Not on your life!" cried Fiona. "It's bad enough to be wandering around in 839 A.D. I'm not going into any story in a raven suit."

Old Biddy Gwynn flashed her silver eyes at Fiona. "You can't escape magic when it's woven all through your life," she stated. "You came to me seeking the answers. Are you going to turn away when they're almost within your grasp?"

Fiona's heart was beating so hard she was afraid it would turn a somersault. She did feel the magic beneath her feet and in the trees. She realized that she desperately wanted to know the story of the red doe. She knew that Bran would never forgive her if she turned back now. More than that, she would never forgive herself for missing this chance.

"O.K.," she whispered at last. "Do it fast, before I change my mind."

"Look closely at the ravens," commanded Biddy. "For you are the ravens!"

11

"Auwk! She wasn't kidding around!" squawked Fiona. "Yeah! She really did it!" cried Bran. "She sure is some powerful Druid."

"She sure is some crazy old coot," said Fiona miserably. "I can't believe I let her talk me into this."

"What do you mean?" crowed Bran. "Didn't you always wish you could fly? Now you can!"

"I can't fly," objected Fiona. "I've never flown in my life, except in airplanes."

"It comes with the bird suit," said Bran. "Look at me."

Fiona opened her eyes a crack to observe Bran making graceful circles through the trees.

"How did you do that?" demanded Fiona.

"Easy. Just let yourself go," Bran urged.

"No, I want to know *how* you did it," insisted Fiona. "Did you start out on your right foot or your left foot? How did you hold your arms—I mean wings?"

"First let go of the tree," Bran suggested.

Fiona unwrapped her wings from the tree trunk and swayed uncertainly on the branch Biddy had seen fit to perch her upon—a branch twelve feet off the ground.

Bran studied his feet. "Well, I guess I kind of hopped and raised my wings at the same time— It's no good, Fiona, you just have to do it."

"Do it for me again, so I can watch," insisted Fiona.

"O.K.," said Bran. He took off, made a circle, and landed neatly beside his sister. "See how easy it is?"

"No," said Fiona, steadying herself against her brother. "And don't wiggle the branch like that. I didn't see what you did with your wings. I was too busy watching your feet. Do it again."

Bran shrugged and flew his little circle one more time. "O.K., now *you* try."

"I think I understand the first part," said Fiona. "But I didn't get what happens when you want to come *down* somewhere. Will you just do it one more time, please?"

"You're such a turkey," cawed Bran in exasperation. "We're supposed to be watching some story and you won't even get off your perch."

"Just once more," pleaded Fiona.

"This is the last time," warned Bran. He made his circle. "Now you do it!" he cried from the air.

"No! I'm scared!"

"Fi-oh-na!" Bran came down hard. The twig twanged. Fiona went tumbling head over claws.

"Eee-ee-ah!"

"Put your wings out, dummy!" Bran yelled.

Fiona spread her wings. It was like opening a parachute. Suddenly, she was floating.

"Jerk! Watch where you're going!"

She opened her eyes just in time to see that she was gliding gracefully into a tree trunk.

"Aaark!" Without thinking, Fiona tipped her wings, barely missing a collision. She landed on her feet, rolled over, and bumped her beak.

"Ow." She sat in the moss, rubbing her beak with her wing.

"You flew! You flew!" cried Bran, landing beside her.

"I fell," said Fiona.

"You fell, but then you flew," insisted her brother. "See how easy it is? C'mon, let's see if we can find that doe." Bran took off, flying low among the trees. He looked back for his sister. There she was, walking sedately over roots and stones.

Bran couldn't help laughing. "You look like a tiny human in a bird suit."

"That's what I am," Fiona insisted. "I think Biddy

gave me a bad set of wings. I try to fly but I can't."
She jiggled her wings feebly.

"Biddy should have turned you into a chicken!"
jeered Bran.

Fiona was thinking of a brilliant retort, when the
ground began to shake. She turned just in time to see an
enormous beast thundering down upon her. Before she
knew it, she was flying, and looking at a red deer running below.

"That's the doe!" Bran was calling. "Follow her!"

Fiona found if she concentrated on following Bran
and the doe and didn't *think* about flying, she did very
well. In fact, after she recovered from her terror, she
was actually beginning to enjoy herself, until she discovered what had been making the doe run so hard.

About fifty ferocious hounds were on her trail, and
they were gaining. Fiona caught up with her brother.
"Do you think the poor little thing is going to get
away?"

"I don't know," said Bran. "See how her tongue is
hanging out? She stumbled back there and almost fell. I
don't think she can hold out much longer."

As if she could hear the ravens speaking, the doe
stopped, panting and wild-eyed, and turned to face her
pursuers.

Two dogs, larger than the rest, charged out of the
pack and rushed the deer.

"I can't look!" cried Fiona.

"Let's go peck their eyes out!" cawed Bran.

But to the McCools' amazement and relief, the two dogs did not attack the doe. Instead, they turned their backs on her and bared their teeth at the rest of the pack.

"They're protecting her!" Bran croaked in disbelief.

The two dogs were circling the doe and keeping all the other dogs at bay.

The doe gave what seemed to the ravens a sigh of relief. She lay down and began licking herself. The two savior dogs appeared to be the leaders of the pack, for the rest stood skulking and growling, but none tried to charge at the little doe.

While one of the dogs stood guard, the other bent down over the doe and began licking her face.

"It's like a fairy tale," murmured Fiona from her perch.

"It is," agreed Bran. "Even the colors are brighter than real." The sun streamed through the trees, gilding the branches as a hundred birds burst into song.

This idyll was broken by the shouts of hunters. In their lead was a man the McCools would have known anywhere.

"Finn!" cawed Bran, forgetting himself entirely. Luckily, his cry came out in raven-language, and Finn was so intent upon the miraculous scene of the doe and the dogs that he missed the shrieking raven entirely.

It was Finn, grown slightly older and broader, but still Finn. The McCools also recognized Goll, Caolite, and bald, scowling Conan, who had once held them prisoner. There were numerous other men, younger men, whom the McCools didn't recognize.

"It's the Fianna," said Fiona, needlessly.

Finn left his men with the pack of skulking dogs and approached the doe. The two protector dogs growled at him. Finn laughed. "Easy there, Bran, Scoelan. I'm not going to hurt your pretty doe."

High on his perch, Bran the raven crowed, "He remembered me! He did! He named his dog after me."

"Big deal," croaked Fiona. "You've got a dog named after you."

Finn put his arm around the doe's neck and with the two protector dogs following, he cleared a way through the pack of slobbering hounds.

Two ravens took off and followed the party at a discreet distance.

The Fianna made their home in the heart of a deep and tangled wood. A ring of earth had been pushed up to form a wall, which was topped by a fence of pointed wooden stakes. The ravens flew over and watched as some women and children ran to greet the returning Fianna.

Fiona looked closely to see if any woman came to kiss the tall, blond leader. To her relief, only a few children approached him, shyly, to pet the doe.

Finn himself led the doe to an enclosure where the animals were kept and saw to it that fresh straw was laid down for her bed. Then he strode off toward what appeared to be the banquet hall.

"Where are you going?" Fiona squawked after her brother.

"I'm going with Finn," he cried back over his shoulder.

"I think we should stay with the doe," she objected.

Finn looked up at the two ravens crying and circling above his head.

"He's getting suspicious," said Fiona. "Let's go back and watch the doe. Finn's not going anyplace. You won't lose him."

Bran reluctantly flew back to the pen. It was frustrating to be so near to Finn and not be able to touch him or talk to him. Bran longed to perch on Finn's broad shoulder and follow him everywhere, but Finn wouldn't know he was Bran, so what was the use?

The doe was restless. She watched after Finn until he disappeared into the banquet hall. She shuffled around in the hay, glanced suspiciously at the other animals—a few stupid sheep and a rather dirty goat who was eyeing her. She put her forelegs up on the woven fence and then she did a peculiar thing. She turned into a woman.

"This is getting really weird," said Bran. For the doe was not just any woman. It was a young, pretty woman, and it was Sadie. It was Sadie, their mother, but yet not their mother, for she was younger, around eighteen, the McCools would have guessed.

"What's *she* doing here?" squawked Fiona indignantly.

The first thing Sadie did was to get out of the pen. She climbed the fence nimbly, leaving the sheep to confer in shocked whispers with the goat.

12

I t's all a fairy tale," said Bran to himself as he flew
after Sadie. She went into a building that was far
more magnificent than anything they had seen in Clonmacnoise. The massive, low wooden roof was carved
with fantastic beasts and heads painted in every color
and highlighted in burnished gold. The ravens perched
in an open window to observe what Sadie would do
next.

The Fianna were sitting around a long narrow table,
gnawing on bones and roaring out songs. The McCools
were used to the way the Fianna ate, but Sadie, standing
in the doorway, was a little overwhelmed by this lusty
gathering. But then she spotted the golden head of
Finn, and threaded her way among the revellers until she
reached his side. A hush fell upon the hall.

Finn stood, blushing at the appearance of this lovely young woman. Fiona suddenly remembered how Finn had grown up all alone in the forest, how truly innocent he was.

"And who might you be?" Finn asked, taking Sadie's hand.

"I am Sabdh," said Sadie, "one of the Everlasting Ones. Fear Doriche the Dark Druid of the Men of Dea wanted me for his bride but I refused. So he put me in the shape of a doe and condemned me to run wild in the wood. The only person who has the power to remove the enchantment is Finn mac Cumhall. As long as I am under his protection, I am safe."

"What a bunch of bull!" cried Fiona, twitching her tail indignantly. "I can't believe Finn would fall for that."

"Shh!" warned Bran. "Remember how Finn used to bring down birds with his slingshot."

But Finn had other things on his mind besides noisy ravens. Giving Sadie a look of pure, burning tenderness, he drew her close to his side.

Fiona tucked her head under her wing, searching for a louse. "I hate these mushy scenes," she muttered into her feathers.

When Fiona pulled her head out, the hall was clean and empty. From the sounds of laughter and music, she guessed that the party had moved outside.

As soon as Fiona saw everyone assembled on the

green, she knew Biddy had changed the scene. There was Sadie, all decked out in an embroidered robe with garlands of flowers in her hair. Fiona didn't need an organ playing the wedding march to tell her what this scene was about.

She flew over to join her brother, who was perched on a rowan branch. "Wait till I tell my friends that I was in my mother's wedding," she joked to her brother. " 'What were you, the flower girl or a bridesmaid?' they'll ask. 'Neither, I was the raven!' " Fiona cackled.

"Shut up, Fiona. This is serious. Ma is marrying Finn. You know what that means, don't you?"

"I'm trying not to think about it," said Fiona, watching the festivities with a raven's appreciation for color. "I mean, Finn's our *friend*. We knew him when he was practically a kid. I don't think I want him to be our father."

"Sometimes you can't see past the end of your own beak," croaked Bran. "If Finn is our father, that means I am the son of Finn mac Cumhall, and if I am Finn's son, then I am the next head of the Fianna!" Bran puffed out his chest.

Fiona felt her raven heart plummet to her tail. She had gone through all this to keep her brother safe until she could get him home again, only to have him discover that he was the son of Finn. He would never go with her now.

"How do you know for sure Finn's your father?" she

asked, grasping for straws. "You're not born yet, you know. Let's wait for the rest of the story." She watched nervously as Finn led Sadie back into the hall.

"Well, don't you want to see the rest of the story?" Bran mocked his sister. She was staring blankly into space as the scene gently dissolved around them.

"I suppose," said Fiona reluctantly.

A strong gust of wind shook the rowan bush impatiently. The birds found themselves blown through an upper-story window.

Snuggled up on a bed of skins were Sadie and Finn, looking so in love that Fiona's heart melted in spite of herself. Between the two lovers was a squalling, red-haired infant.

Finn was looking at this baby with pride. "She's loud," he said. "I like that. A fine strong voice."

"What do you want to call her?" asked Sadie. "Please, not one of those long unpronounceable names."

"Fiona," said Finn decisively.

"Fiona? Why Fiona?"

"After a girl—"

"A girl!" huffed Sadie.

Finn smiled and kissed Sadie on the brow. "A *little* girl," he said. "A poet. When I first saw you, you reminded me of her."

"All right," said Sadie a little dubiously.

"Fiona!" Finn raised his infant daughter above his

head. She howled, waving arms and legs. "She's going to be a warrior!" said Finn proudly.

"She's going to have her breakfast," said Sadie firmly, reaching for the child.

"How sweet!" cooed Fiona on the rafter, as much as a raven can coo. "He named his baby after me." She was beginning to like the idea of having Finn for her father. She felt like cuddling up to him, putting her head inside his ear, and saying, "Hi, Daddy, it's me, Fiona." Except she knew it would come out "Pruk, pruk, tok!"

"O.K.," grumbled Bran. "Enough of the mushy parts. When are we going to get a little action?"

As if Biddy had only been waiting for her cue, the ravens suddenly found the chamber empty, but there was a great deal of commotion outside on the green.

"This is more like it," cried Bran circling over the Fianna as they assembled in the middle of the fort. They were heavily armed and looked as if they were going to be gone for a long time. Finn stood at their head, proud and tall, not entirely concealing his excitement at being about to embark on an adventure with the Fianna.

"No!" cawed Fiona. "He can't go!"

"What do you expect him to do, stay home and play patty-cake with his baby all the time?" argued Bran. "The Fianna protect Ireland. He's got to fight some-time."

"I know that," said Fiona. "I just have this feeling that he shouldn't go—"

"But you know I have to go when the enemy attacks—" Finn was explaining to Sadie.

"I know," Sadie said tearfully. "I only wish you didn't look so happy."

Finn gave her a wounded look. "Happy? I'm miserable at leaving you and the baby. Have I ever left your side since you came to me that night?"

Sadie shook her head.

"And I wouldn't now," said Finn self-righteously, "if Ireland didn't need me." He kissed her goodbye again. "One thing you must promise me, my gentle Sabdh. Promise me you won't put even a foot outside the fort until I come back."

"And where do you think I'd go? Out chasing after a wild boar?" Sadie gestured toward the woods surrounding the fort.

"Promise me," urged Finn.

"I promise."

There was more tearful kissing and leave-taking, which Bran thought would never end, until at last Finn strode off at the head of his men.

"Finn! Finn!" screamed Fiona. "Don't go! Something terrible is going to happen!"

"Shut up," croaked Bran. "He knows what he's doing."

* * *

Fiona sat in the window of the great hall, watching with interest as two women sewed beneath her. Everything looked cheerful and innocent enough. Why did she have this terrible foreboding?

Bran blew in beside her, looking frazzled.

"What happened to you?" asked Fiona.

"I was trying to follow Finn when the whole Fianna disappeared in a mist and I got caught in a tornado or something. I guess Old Biddy Gwynn wants me to watch these ladies sewing instead of Finn going to battle." He began to sulk.

"Well, if it makes you feel any better, I have goose bumps, or raven bumps, all over my body," said Fiona, ruffling her beard. "I feel like I'm watching one of those movies where everything looks all right, but there's this creepy music playing in the background and you know something's going to happen." She cocked her head to listen to what the sewing ladies were saying.

"How is the lady?" one of them was asking the other.

"Still sighing and mooning about," replied her companion.

"You told her he won't be back for a long time, didn't you?"

"Yes, but you know these young wives the first time their husbands go to battle—"

Right on cue, the door opened and Sadie walked into the hall, trailed by a plump little girl, about two years old, with red curly hair. It wasn't exactly the same Sadie as in the last scene, because this Sadie had a swollen belly.

"Boy, did she get fat!" cawed Bran.

"She's not fat, you dodo, she's pregnant," croaked Fiona.

"Pregnant!" Bran looked at Sadie with more interest. "With me! Well, I guess that's proof, if anything is," he clucked with a satisfied air. "What beats me is why Ma ever left Finn."

The sewing ladies were getting annoyed with this raven conversation going on above them. One stood up to shoo the noisy birds away when her attention was distracted by a muffled sob. It was Sadie, standing in an open doorway at the end of the hall. Her little child was clinging to her cloak.

The sewing ladies hurried over to her. "Now, now, there's no use looking for him. The battle's far off in the west. Sometimes they're gone a year—"

The ravens flew to the doorway and perched on a rafter. Sadie was looking west, across a plain that had been cleared on one side of the fort. A few pigs were rooting beside a narrow dirt track.

Suddenly, Sadie gave a sharp cry. "He's here! He's back!"

The sewing ladies looked at each other. The ravens on the rafter exchanged a quizzical glance, then peered down the path. There was nothing there, only the pigs and, maybe, a play of shadows on the edge of the wood.

But Sadie was already running through the gates of the fort and across the plain, her arms outstretched. The baby toddled after, chortling.

"Come back!" called the sewing ladies. "Where are you galloping off to?"

"Dummy! Didn't Finn tell you not to leave the fort?" shrieked Fiona.

But Sadie seemed not to hear either the women or the screaming raven over her head. "Finn, my own!" she was crying. The ravens were sure she'd gone crazy, for they couldn't see anyone there.

But then, as Sadie reached the edge of the wood, a shadow, as thin as a knife, leaped out at her. Sadie cried, "No, no!" The shadow passed over her and there was a red doe standing in her place with a rope around her neck.

The startled animal balked and fought as the shadowy thing dragged her off into the wood. The little girl followed at her heels, whimpering.

13

The apparition led the doe on through ever darkening woods. The little girl had long ago fallen in exhaustion, and since the doe refused to leave her child, she had been allowed to carry her on her back. Two black ravens followed as closely as they dared.

Now they were winding down into a cold, dark glen, where the wind blew up from its very depths, slowing the ravens' flight, but still they persevered after the doe, the child, and the thing that held them prisoner.

As it penetrated deeper into the glen, this thing began to take on substance, until it looked like a tall man in a hooded cape. The ravens flew ahead to see his face, but all they saw were deeper shadows within the hood. Behind the doe, close to her heels, there appeared two shadowy hounds. The little child dozed on her mother's back.

The figure was leading the doe to a cave in the side of the glen. "This is your home, my gentle Sabdh," he whispered with hollow breath—or was it the wind? "It's a secret place, wound round with enchantment. You cannot leave. Not even Finn can find you. Now, will you be my bride?" The rope fell from the doe's neck.

The doe shook her head vigorously and backed into a far corner of the cave. The wind laughed. "Not now? But sometime, my beauty. Until you consent to be Fear Doriche's queen and live in a palace of gold, you shall be Fear Doriche's doe and live in a cold stone cave."

The wind moaned through the loathsome glen and the shadows flew away in a chuckling gale.

The doe peered timidly out of the mouth of the cave, then drew back with a shudder. She made herself a bed of leaves in the rear of the cave, lay down carefully and coaxed the little girl off her back, who slept on without a murmur. The doe sighed and curled her body around the child. Then she, too, fell asleep.

The ravens huddled together, blinking back tears at this sad turn of events.

"So *that* was Fear Doriche the Dark Druid of the Men of Dea," said Fiona. "And I thought Ma had made it all up. I wondered how she got mixed up with him. He doesn't seem like her type."

"He's not my type either," said Bran. "Boy, you and Ma are sure in some mess."

"What do you mean, me and Ma?" asked Fiona.

"You're in this too. Ma was pregnant when Fear Doriche did his dirty deed. Remember?"

"Oh, yeah. I wonder if I'll be born a deer—"

As if Biddy Gwynn were backstage working the
lights, the darkness disappeared and the cave was bathed
in a warm, soft glow.

The doe and the little girl were where they had last
been, but they had been joined by a rosy, naked baby
boy.

"Oh, brother," croaked Bran.

"Aw, you were cute, Bran," cooed Fiona. "Listen,
she's singing you a lullaby."

If the McCools had been in their human shape, they
never could have heard the doe's song, but their enchanted shape let them understand other animals. When
the doe had finished, she nuzzled her baby and said, "I
think I'll call you Bran, after the dog who saved my
life." She began bathing him with her tongue.

Bran the raven was thinking he'd fly out for a little
exercise when a cold wind blew in. The doe nudged her
children behind her and faced the opening, her head
lowered. The ravens fluttered up to a hidden rock ledge.

An eddy of leaves swirled and settled at the feet of a
cruel shadow. The doe lowered her head threateningly.
Mocking laughter echoed through the cave.

Then the whispering began: "Will you come, my
beauty? Will you be Fear Doriche's queen? Will you?

Will you? . . ." The whispering went on, describing in detail the glories of Fear Doriche's kingdom under the ground.

Finally, a meek, submissive look came into the doe's eyes. She nodded yes. Two ravens nearly fell off their ledge. Now the cave rang with triumphant shouts, and the doe was once more a beautiful young woman, the gentle Sabdh, or Sadie, as she was known to some.

Instantly, Sadie snatched up her baby and wrapped him in her cloak. The little girl clung to her legs.

"Leave them!" hissed an icy voice.

"No," said Sadie defiantly. "If I go, they go, too."

Fiona the raven was not at all sure she wanted Fiona the baby to go traipsing off after her new stepfather, Fear Doriche the Dark Druid of the Men of Dea, but even if Fiona could have figured out how to stop them, she remembered that she was watching a story, and probably nothing she could do would change it.

And so the long march out of the cursed glen began, the dark wind leading the way, followed by the captive Sadie carrying her baby with her little red-haired girl tripping behind. Two anxious ravens brought up the rear.

As a poet, Fiona was surprised that Biddy was letting the walk go on for so long. Poor Sadie was getting wretchedly weary, to say nothing of little Fiona, who was whimpering and falling at every step. Baby Bran was howling with hunger, and still the band trooped on.

The sun was going down on this seemingly endless day when Sadie said, "Fear Doriche, you were right. I can't go another step dragging these children. Let me put them in this boat and send them out to the middle of the lake, where they'll be safe. I'll come get them tomorrow on one of those red horses you promised me."

The ravens looked ahead. Sure enough, there was a lake, all silver and pink in the light of the setting sun, and at the edge, loosely tied to a tree, was a long dugout canoe.

"That birdbrain," squawked Fiona. "Does she honestly imagine that Fear Doriche is going to let her come back for us?"

"Shh!" said Bran. "Let's see what happens."

Sadie had taken off her cloak and was wrapping her baby in it. She stepped into the canoe and laid her bundle tenderly on the bottom. Next she reached out for the little girl and brought her into the craft with them. But the little girl didn't want her mother to leave her. She cried and held her mother tightly. Sadie tried to free herself, but the child only clung all the more. Little by little, the commotion the mother and child were making in the canoe began to free it from its moorings. They were drifting out into the lake.

Sadie was quietly, insistently, talking to her child. The ravens flew overhead, trying to hear.

"It's the chant!" whispered Bran finally. "She's reciting the Druid chant!"

The ravens looked nervously toward shore, but the shadow was leaning casually against a young alder tree.

Bran the raven took up the chant, crowing along with Sadie. Slowly, the heavy craft began turning in the water.

Fiona saw the shadow by the tree stiffen. "He must have heard Bran," she decided. The edge of the lake turned black. Whirlpool ripples appeared on the reddening water. The canoe turned faster and faster.

A blast of wind howled and raged on shore. The boat spun, light as a stick. The ravens found themselves whirling helplessly above. They fought their way up out of the turbulence.

Now the very rocks around the shore were throbbing with dark Druid curses, but the boat spun ever faster. The ravens flew higher.

The water rose around the canoe in a funnel, making the air rise around the water, forcing the ravens up, up, ever higher. The birds, swirling helplessly, looked far down to see a column of water in the middle of the lake. When at last it subsided, the canoe was gone.

14

For a long time, Fiona flew after her brother, with no thought as to where they were going. The steady beat of her wings helped calm her as she went over all the surprising things she had learned.

Sadie had had her own part to play in the Legend of Finn. Not in her most inventive daydreams would Fiona have imagined *this*. Her mother had never even hinted— Still, Fiona realized, if Sadie had told her outright that she had married Finn, she never would have believed her. Sadie seemed too much a mother to have had an adventure like that.

Finn was her father, and Bran's. And yet, she and Bran, on their first adventure into the Legend of Finn, had known him when he was practically still a boy. "That's where time-traveling can really mess you up," thought Fiona, surprising herself by doing a lazy loop-the-loop in the sky.

Fiona remembered what Uncle Rupert had told her about how Sadie had been discovered, with her children, sitting in a canoe high on the wall of a museum in Dublin. If ravens could smile, Fiona would have, to think of her clever mother taking her children time-traveling in a canoe.

She and Bran were wizard children. They belonged to two times. Perhaps they belonged to all times. Fiona had been afraid she would discover this. Strangely enough, now that she knew it, she wasn't afraid anymore. She even liked the idea of having Finn for a father. But Bran was another problem altogether. What would he do when Biddy changed them back to their human forms? Probably go straight to Finn. It was so confusing and worrying that Fiona was glad, for the moment, that she was a raven. Otherwise she'd be getting a headache.

Now that she thought of it, where was Biddy? Fiona pushed a little harder to catch up with Bran.

"Bran," she said, coming alongside him, "don't you think Biddy should have changed the scene, or brought us home, or something by now?"

"Oh, you're quick, Fiona, quick," mocked Bran. "I've been thinking that since Ma disappeared in the canoe. Obviously, Biddy should have brought us back as soon as the story was over."

Fiona thought she might be getting airsick. She now recalled that Biddy had been a dragonfly for two hundred years. If she hadn't been able to change *herself* back. . . . Maybe she was terrific at changing people into animals, but when it came to changing them back, she messed up.

Fiona pictured Old Biddy Gwynn and her jug of mead. Then again, maybe she had only forgotten about them temporarily.

"Shouldn't we go down and roost in a tree by the lake or something?" Fiona suggested. "If Biddy *is* looking for us, she's never going to find us flapping around up here."

"It's a little late to think of that."

"What do you mean?"

"We've been flying all night."

Fiona blinked into the drizzle. Now that Bran mentioned it, it *was* day, and they had started flying at sunset. "You mean we've been flying around like a couple of lost loons all night?" she shrieked.

"We're not lost," Bran insisted. "I've been following the river, hoping it would take us back to Clonmacnoise."

Fiona glanced down at the black ribbon unfurling through woods and bogs. "That could be the right river," she said, "although they all look the same to me. But I'd like to point out to you that you and I are about eight hundred years too early to find Clonmacnoise. Biddy sent us back in time, remember?"

"She sent us into a legend," said Bran, splitting hairs. "That was a very strong spell Ma was doing. I don't know where it took her, but after she was gone I felt like we had broken out of the legend. All the enchantment was gone. Things looked more real. So on a hunch, I flew in the direction where I thought the river might be, and when I found the river—"

"Of all the dumb schemes," Fiona croaked. She was too weak to shriek. It was bad enough not knowing *where* she was, but not knowing *when* she was, and having a raven body on top of it all, that was more than Fiona could handle.

"How long do you think we've been away?" she asked, desperately applying logic to an illogical situation.

Bran tried figuring it out with her, but they ended up being completely flummoxed. With the way Biddy had kept changing the scene, they could have been gone hours, days, weeks, or even years.

Bran persuaded Fiona to keep following the river. Fiona complied because anything else would have been giving up. She flew on, trying not to think about being a raven lost in a strange, wild land.

For the first time since she had changed her shape, Fiona felt hungry. "Bran, let's check out that big rock. It looks like a place where we could get out of the rain for a while, and there might be a soft little mouse hiding in one of the crevices. Ugh! What did I say?"

When the ravens flew around to the other side of the rock, they found the opening to a nice dry cave.

"This place looks familiar," said Fiona, wondering if she should look for mice, and if she found one, if she could eat it. Suddenly, she realized where they were. "This is Old Biddy Gwynn's front parlor!"

The ravens looked around the cave. It was bare as a bone and showed no signs of having been a dwelling place.

"Do you think it's after or before she lived here?" asked Fiona. " 'Cause she sure isn't here now."

"Hey, look at that," said Bran, strutting up and down. "Bran, son of Finn, does it again. I got you to Clonmacnoise, didn't I? Huh? Admit it. I did it."

"O.K., O.K.," granted Fiona. "We're in the right place, but are we in the right time?"

"There's only one way to find out," cawed Bran, taking off in the direction of Clonmacnoise.

Fiona took one last look around for mice and flew after her brother.

"Ladies and gentlemen, out the window to your right," Bran called after a few minutes, "you'll see the city of Clonmacnoise."

The McCools soared over the monastery wall and perched on the edge of the covered well to get their bearings.

"It all looks the same to me," said Bran.

"So where's that old quack of a Druid?" asked Fiona, shaking her feathers.

"Maybe we should look for Legaire," suggested Bran.

"That's right. Let's go find Legaire," crowed Fiona. She suddenly realized how much she missed Legaire's cheerful, easy ways. He would know what to do. Thinking of Legaire reminded her of the sacred trout. She threw a casual look over her shoulder to see if they were still swimming in the well. She stopped and turned around, peering intently into the water.

"Checking to see if your feathers are on straight before you meet Legaire?" teased Bran. He put his head next to hers. Then his beak dropped open. He saw the reflection of two ravens and above their heads, circling in the water, two white oblong shapes.

The ravens gaped at the fish, slowly revolving, white bellies up, in the dark water.

"Maybe the water went bad. Maybe they were overfed," Fiona suggested hopefully.

"Maybe," said Bran. "Come on. Let's go."

The McCools rose in a circle around the city and hovered over the harbor. Their raven eyes were attracted to bright things bobbing in the water. They folded their wings and dropped down for a closer look.

The bright things were the brilliantly striped sails of long boats, their high curving prows carved to look like snarling beasts. Bran perched on the curling upper lip of one such beast. He scanned the length of the empty vessel. It looked oddly familiar—the narrow high sail, the long oars on either side. Bran closed his eyes for a moment and remembered a picture in one of his comic books of a boat like this one, on rough seas, with mighty bearded men wearing horned helmets straining at the oars.

"Vikings!" cried Bran.

"Outsiders!" Fiona called at the same time from her perch on the bow.

"The Outsiders are Vikings!"

Bran thought of all he'd ever learned about Vikings. Legaire said the Outsiders came from the north. Vikings came from the north. But they weren't cowards. Far from it. They were some of the greatest, most feared warriors of all time. Part of Bran was thrilled. He was going to see real Vikings. Part of him froze. What would the Vikings do to Clonmacnoise?

The oars creaked in their sockets. Bran fought back a raven curiosity which made him want to explore the empty ships.

"The Vikings have come!" he shrilled to Fiona.

Cawing in alarm, the ravens wheeled over the city. In answer to their cries came the blast of war trumpets. The Vikings had entered the city, and they were not there on a social call.

15

When the McCools flew over the city and took their first look at the Vikings, their hearts sank. "It's like a pro team against the high school all-stars," observed Bran.

Fiona had to agree it was true. The men, women, and children of Clonmacnoise were armed with wooden shovels, hunting knives, and an occasional sword. The Vikings were equipped with long swords, bows and arrows, murderous looking battle-axes, and daggers. As if this weren't enough, the Vikings were protected by helmets and shields.

The ravens shrieked as the Vikings swarmed over the wall that Bran had predicted would be useless under attack, and went sweeping into the city, mowing down all who stood in their way. Beneath the frantically darting ravens, the Vikings plundered and murdered. A contingent was heading purposefully for the monastery. The ravens followed.

The walls of the monastery, although lower than those of the city, were more carefully built, and the monks had been able to close the solid-oak gates. The McCools could see the monks standing guard on top of the wall, armed with rocks and slingshots. Legaire, Connor the Culdee, and Angus stood shoulder to shoulder by the main gate. Behind them, but where he could still get a good view of the action, was Uncle Rupert.

"Uncle Rupert!" called Fiona. "Get down! You don't know anything about fighting." But Uncle Rupert was so captivated by the sight of the Vikings that he didn't notice the raven calling to him.

"They don't know who we are," Fiona realized. "They'll all be killed and we'll have to spend the rest of our lives as ravens." An arrow split the air, just missing Uncle Rupert. Fiona forgot herself in her concern for her uncle.

Bran was still on the Viking side of the wall, frantically beating the air with his wings. "If only Finn was here," he heard himself cry. As he said this he realized that it would be hard to imagine Finn, the fairy-tale prince from his gilded woods, here in the mud and stones and blood of Clonmacnoise. No, Finn was a legend and an inspiration. He didn't belong here.

Bran looked at Legaire, fighting from the top of the ramparts. The son of Finn, belonged here fighting beside his friend. Bran had never felt more himself, even in his raven shape.

Bran saw a Viking raise his spear, preparing to hurl it at Legaire. With a shriek, he aimed himself at the Viking and sunk his talons into his big red nose.

The warrior swatted him, sending him to the ground.

"Bran!" cried Legaire, reaching down. Bran grabbed his hand and scrambled to the top of the wall.

The Viking blow had broken the enchantment and given Bran back his human shape. Legaire grinned at him and tossed him the sword he'd used in practice. "I was hoping you'd come," he said, as if Bran had walked in late to a party.

Fiona started at the sight of her brother, standing on the ramparts. "Of course," she said to herself. "In those old legends, a lot of times a blow changes the enchanted animal back to human shape!" What a relief! If worst came to worst, she could always provoke a Viking into hitting her and changing her back to Fiona the girl. For the moment, however, she preferred the body of a raven. She decided to be a spy and report to Bran on what was happening down in the city.

The news she had to relate was not good. "They've rounded up a lot of women and kids and have them tied up in the boats. The city is burning. They're collecting silver and gold and even cooking pots, and putting them in the boats, too. It looks like they're going to clean out the city and then come after the monastery."

Fiona delivered her message and flew away, speechless with grief. She had just had a vision of the future. She saw Bran, Uncle Rupert, Legaire, Angus, and all of Clonmacnoise destroyed by Vikings. Over this desolation flew a lone raven, keening her heart out. Fiona flew to the little church and landed on the windowsill.

Minutes passed before the raven saw anything. Then her eye lit on something, something she had never seen in the church before, but which was as familiar to her as her own claw. It was a large, leather-covered book, one the raven remembered from another time—a time when she was a red-haired girl.

"Uncle Rupert's magic book!" crowed Fiona. It could be no other. The only difference between this and the book she had pored over in Uncle Rupert's library was that this one was newer, by about a thousand years.

"That's what Uncle Rupert and Angus must have been working on all this time," Fiona realized, recalling the pointed letters her uncle had been drawing so carefully. "That's why the book didn't come with us from home. It was already here." If Fiona could have, she would have burst into song like a canary. They could all escape! They could all go home!

"Of course, we have to wait for a magic night,"

Fiona told herself, "and we have to get this book out past the Vikings, because Legaire said the Outsiders destroy the books. They hate the books." As Fiona babbled on to herself, she remembered the underground passage Legaire had told them about, the one he'd escaped through when he was a little boy. If they could find that passage, they'd be home free!

Fiona went swooping back over the city to check on the enemy, and saw that her prediction was already coming true. A whole new mass of Vikings was swarming up the hill.

She spotted her brother and landed on his shoulder. "We're outnumbered," she panted. "Hundreds of Vikings—coming now. But we're in luck. I found the magic book. It's inside the church! Can you believe it? Uncle Rupert and Angus were working on it right under our noses. There's no time to lose. Ask Legaire where that passage is, the one he took when he was a little kid. We can bring Legaire and Angus home with us. Ma won't mind."

Bran looked at Fiona as if she were mad. "Legaire can't run. He's an O'Kelley. The O'Kelleys are sworn to defend Clonmacnoise."

"But this is different. These are Vikings! We're way outnumbered."

"He's sworn to defend Clonmacnoise *to the death*. You know what that means, don't you?"

Fiona preferred not to think what it meant. There was no time. She could hear the enemy at the wall. "Well then, you and Uncle Rupert—"

"I'm not running either," said Bran stubbornly. "The son of Finn does not run."

Fiona opened her beak to shout, "You're Sadie's son, too," but she closed it. She thought of the brave woman who had lived as a doe in a cave and had given birth to a son all alone rather than surrender to the Dark Druid. Would that Sadie tell her son to escape and leave his friend to fight the Vikings? For once, Fiona didn't have an answer.

It seemed the harder she tried to make sure Bran came home with her, the more she failed. She had helped Bran find his father, only to discover it was Finn. The reason she had helped Bran find his father was to keep him from fighting, and now he was going to fight anyway. If he was lucky enough to survive the Vikings, he'd only go back to Finn.

"It's all Ma's fault," thought Fiona. "If she'd leveled with me in the first place, we never would have fallen into this mess." Fiona's only hope now was that if Bran came out of the battle alive, she might be able to get him to go back and see Sadie one last time. Then let *her* worry about Bran.

"At least," she begged, "persuade Uncle Rupert to escape. He can take the magic book and some of the other treasures with him. He's not doing anyone any good here."

Bran looked at his uncle rushing to and fro, getting in everyone's way, and he realized Fiona was right.

"Legaire." Bran turned to his friend. "Fiona here thinks Uncle Rupert should try to escape with the book and other treasures. Where is that secret passage? Would it take him past the Vikings?"

For the first time, Legaire noticed the raven on Bran's shoulder. "Fiona! Is that you? What won't you Mac Cools think of next? I should have known; you're much too pretty for an ordinary raven." He thought for a moment. "Yes, I think he could get past them that way, although I don't know if it's even open anymore. Look over there. It should be under those gorse bushes."

It was easy to convince Uncle Rupert that the raven on Bran's shoulder was Fiona. It was not so easy, however, to persuade him that he should flee with the book. It wasn't until Fiona told Bran to tell him that it was his *mission* to save the book that Uncle Rupert agreed.

"He's not really brave," thought Fiona, flying after her uncle. "He's just so curious, he forgets about danger."

Her thoughts were interrupted by a roar. She darted back to the wall and saw the enemy charging the gates with an enormous log. Uncle Rupert had heard too and was hobbling over to investigate. Fiona screamed at him and beat his face with her wings, driving him back toward the church. She didn't think the gates would hold long now.

While Uncle Rupert was collecting treasure from the church, Fiona hopped around under the gorse bushes by the north wall. Finally, she spied some loose stones. She flew out of the bushes and saw Uncle Rupert limping toward her with a sack over his shoulder.

Although Fiona couldn't make her uncle understand her raven speech, he understood her signals, and was soon on his knees, scrabbling among the loose stones.

"Good heavens! A souterrain! Legaire was right!" Uncle Rupert had uncovered a man-sized hole. "But how does he expect me to get through there? It's diabolically dark."

The hole was dark, but not too dark for raven eyes. Fiona longed to get back to the battle and watch over Bran and Legaire, but she saw that she was going to have to lead her uncle through the tunnel.

"There's air coming from somewhere," said Fiona to herself as she fluttered down five feet. The tunnel was too low for Uncle Rupert to stand. He had to crawl, dragging his bag of treasure behind.

Fiona flew in short little hops. "This is more a job for a bat than a bird," she grumbled.

The tunnel, although low, was mercifully short. It ended right outside the north wall. Fiona emerged first and looked around anxiously for stray Vikings, but they all seemed to be occupied elsewhere.

"It's safe!" she called to Uncle Rupert. He squeezed through the opening, which had been carefully concealed in a thicket of blackberry bushes.

Fiona led her uncle on over the bog to the Druid grove where Old Biddy Gwynn had worked her magic. Fiona half-expected to see Biddy there, napping under a tree, but there were only the oaks, looking wise and serene, far from the events taking place at Clonmacnoise. Fiona settled briefly into one of them to catch her breath.

A jackdaw, sitting on the branch above, winked at her. Fiona gasped. Now that she was in an enchanted shape, she understood. The jackdaw was really a Druid.

"The Vikings are attacking the monastery," she said urgently.

The bird shrugged. "You think *that's* a battle. You should have been there when the men of Ulster met the men of Leinster at Rosnaree. There was a fight!"

"I just thought if you, and maybe some of the other jackdaws sitting around in the trees here, wanted to help, we might be able to save the monastery—"

From all around came the high nasal tittering of jackdaws. "Why should we want to save those bell-clanging clerics?" asked one of them.

"Well, they *are* Irish—" Fiona offered.

Again, more laughter from the jackdaw audience.

"Miserable fighters. They're not Irish to me," said the first jackdaw, blinking his yellow eyes at Fiona.

Fiona could see she wasn't going to get anywhere with these haughty jackdaws.

"At least take care of Uncle Rupert," she croaked and flew back toward the city.

16

The monks did their best, but rocks, spears, and even buckets of boiling oatmeal poured on their heads could not turn back the relentless Vikings. Again and again, the attackers charged forward with their battering ram. The oak doors shuddered, then splintered, then shattered. With a mighty shout, the enemy swarmed into the monastery.

The monks of Clonmacnoise were waiting for them on the green in front of the church. Legaire and Bran stood in the front row. Bran braced himself as the helmeted hoard thundered up the hill.

"Death to the heathen!" came a cry from behind. Connor the Culdee charged out of the group, a battle-axe held high. Connor's axe sent the head of the first Viking rolling back down the hill, and the fight was on.

"This one looks big enough for two!" called Legaire to Bran. "I'll take the top. You take the bottom."

Bran slashed out at the same time as Legaire, sending the large Viking to a speedy end. The system worked so well that Legaire and Bran decided to work in tandem when they could. It seemed Bran was just small enough that the big warriors tended to overlook him. While Legaire distracted them, Bran could come up from below and drive his sword home.

To Bran, it was as if the blood of every man he vanquished were surging into his veins, giving him more strength. He twirled and slashed his way through the Vikings like a maddened dwarf. With Legaire beside him, he felt as if he could take on the entire Viking nation.

Fiona, from her vantage point as a raven, was getting a whole other view of the battle. She saw that only a small part of the Viking army was engaged in fighting the last remnant of monks on the hill. The rest were still occupied with taking everything they could from the smoldering ruins of Clonmacnoise. They were loading sheep on one boat, women and children on another. Sacks of treasure were filling a third.

All through the city, the white bodies of the fallen defenders of Clonmacnoise lay in the mud and the drizzle. With a dread-filled heart, the raven flew over the monastery wall, looking for her brother and Legaire.

Miraculously, they were still alive. Fiona opened her beak to give a cry of encouragement, but it stuck in her craw. Bran and Legaire were whooping it up like scouts at a jamboree, while they sliced a man to death.

Fiona dive-bombed behind a bush and rolled moaning in the dirt. Of all she had seen this was the worst. Bran talked big about defending Clonmacnoise and not deserting a friend, but when it came down to it, he was actually enjoying himself. He was having fun killing other human beings! At last it was clear to her that Bran couldn't be saved. He had turned into someone different. So let him. Let him live in the ancient forest, or here in Clonmacnoise, happily hacking off people's heads until he died at an early age. She would go back to the Druid grove and wait for this butchery to be over.

Fiona tried not to look again, but she couldn't help flying over for one last farewell circle. Bran and Legaire had their separate challengers now, and a brutal looking warrior was coming up behind Bran with an axe.

Without stopping to think, Fiona screamed and flew at Bran's attacker, pecking his eyes savagely and making him drop his weapon. Bran dispatched his sword into the first Viking's bowels, pulled it out with a wrench, and stabbed at the howling blinded warrior behind him.

Fiona spat the taste of Viking blood from her beak. She'd done it. She was as guilty as Bran. There was no thought of going back to the Druid grove now. Fiona hadn't any choice but to see the battle out to its grim conclusion. Unlike Bran, she did not feel invincible. She felt certain that they would all be killed, for she had seen the enemy.

Still, Fiona fought, with the weapons of a raven—beak, wings, and claws. She lost count of how many Vikings she helped cut down. So engrossed was she in her work, she didn't notice that the sun was pulling away from the sight of this brutal day. The fires of Clonmacnoise were dying. Viking horns began bellowing from the harbor.

It was some time before the last remaining bloodied defenders of Clonmacnoise realized the enemy was leaving.

"They're going!" cheered Bran. "We beat them!" He ran to look out over the wall. Fiona perched on his shoulder.

"Beat them," she said bitterly. "Sure, look around you, pal. They took Clonmacnoise with them and left us nothing but corpses."

Bran turned. The monastery of Clonmacnoise was a hideous, blackened skeleton. He picked his way up the hill to where the church had stood, as if he were seeing it all for the first time. Fiona was right. There was nothing left.

His thoughts were shattered by the harsh scream of a raven. The bird was sitting on the chest of a fallen boy, a boy with a face so white it seemed like silver, and hair as black as the raven's own feathers. Beneath him, blood was darkly oozing and mingling with the mud.

Bran rushed to close Legaire's wound with his hands, but the blood came up thick and fast between his fingers.

"Ah, you can't keep the life in me, Bran," sighed Legaire. "Don't try. Give me your hand before I leave."

Bran pressed his bloodied hand into Legaire's.

"Is this Fiona?" The other white hand fluttered up and landed softly on the raven. "Come, put your head against my cheek."

Making herself as soft as the silk from a milkweed pod, Fiona roosted on Legaire's shoulder.

A smile flickered across the dying boy's face. "I feel very light. Lighter than you, Fiona. I'm leaving soon. Stay with me through the night. Help me find my way."

The three friends were still. Then the raven felt a long breath rattle past the bone-white lips that were once so red.

"Bran," she coughed. "Hit me and make me human. This raven's heart can't hold the sorrow."

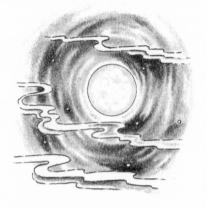

17

Sorrow. It was the first time Fiona had ever used the word. Now, with a swollen human heart, she sat in the mud with Legaire's head in her lap. Bran sat beside her. Silently they watched moon shadows cross their dead friend's face.

During the night, Angus, taut and pale, came to crouch at Legaire's feet. Somehow he had rescued the harp. He placed it on his knee and began singing one after another of Legaire's songs. As he sang of the beautiful lands in the west where brave warriors went to live forever under roofs thatched with wings of birds, Fiona imagined Legaire's spirit lightly rising from his body to go to that land. She hoped he would meet Finn there and they would sing the old songs together.

The next thing Fiona knew, it was morning, and

Connor the Culdee was standing over them. Fiona started, but Connor seemed to have forgotten his feud with her. He knelt down and wrapped his dead cousin in his cloak. "He has won the martyr's crown," he said in a voice as dry as pebbles.

Fiona and Bran helped Connor and Angus bury Legaire in a grave dug in the ashes of the church.

"We'll build another church over him," said Connor. "To Saint Legaire, the Martyr of Clonmacnoise. We'll build it out of stone, and beside it, a tall tower. A tall tower," he went on, becoming inspired, "that will say to the heathen, 'You cannot crush us. We will not bow before your gods.'"

Fiona looked around. There were many who had won the martyr's crown. Burials were taking place all over the hill. In a day, Clonmacnoise had turned from a city of the living to a monument to the dead.

Connor was warming to his subject—how Clonmacnoise would rise from its ashes and become a beacon to a benighted world. Fiona and Bran were wondering how they could politely leave. For to them, Legaire had gone from his body last night. They were sure he wasn't waiting around to listen to Connor give him a funeral oration.

As Connor went on, a soft breeze came off the river that smelled of budding leaves and dappled sun.

"What time of the year is this?" wondered Fiona aloud.

"Let's go find your Uncle Rupert and ask him," said Angus. "He's very good at dates." He put an arm around each McCool and left Connor the Culdee preaching to the breeze.

They hadn't gone far when they met Uncle Rupert, who was coming back to find them. "There you are," he said, as if he were picking them up after a double feature instead of a battle. "Vikings gone? Well, they'll be back."

"When?" asked Fiona, looking around.

Uncle Rupert laughed. "Oh, not today, I expect. But they'll be in and out for the next two hundred years."

"Two hundred years!" Fiona thought of the bodies lying in the rain.

"What do they teach you in that school besides puppetry and pottery?" asked Uncle Rupert. "Surely you've heard of the Battle of Clontarf, when Brian Boru conquers the Vikings for good in 1014. Not that the invasion of the Vikings is such a bad thing in the long run," said Uncle Rupert, trying to comfort the stricken Fiona. "The Vikings bring trade and establish cities in Ireland. The Irish convert the Vikings to Christianity—"

"How can you say it's not such a bad thing when Legaire is lying in the ground?" Fresh tears came to Fiona's eyes.

Uncle Rupert blinked, as if he hadn't seen until then that Legaire wasn't with them. "Oh. I am sorry." He sighed and laid a hand on Fiona's shoulder. "That's the problem with history, isn't it? How we get caught up in the pageant, forced to play out our roles."

They walked in silence, each one thinking over what Uncle Rupert had said.

Bran tried not to look at the bodies of the unburied Vikings for fear that he'd recognize someone he had killed. During the night, watching Legaire's body, he realized that he had brought men to their death. He had done it because it had seemed wrong to leave a friend in need. But it was wrong to kill, too. Now he was sick of fighting. He was relieved when Angus and Uncle Rupert left Clonmacnoise and began leading them over the bog toward the Druid grove.

"Angus," said Uncle Rupert, when they were at last beyond the smell of death and ashes. "I know you O'Kelleys are sworn to protect Clonmacnoise, but I wonder if you could stretch the vow a little to include the manuscripts of Clonmacnoise. I rescued as many as I could get my hands on. How about leaving Connor here to protect the physical Clonmacnoise while we flee to France with the spirit of Clonmacnoise, as it is embodied in those priceless manuscripts? I hear the court of Charles the Bald is a most congenial place for Irish scribes."

Angus smiled for the first time that day. "Wonderful

idea, Rupert, especially since my saintly cousin is talking as if he means to build numerous stone towers at Clonmacnoise. I don't much take to stonecutting, I'm afraid. I'd rather make my monuments with pen and brush."

"Uh, Uncle Rupert," said Fiona. "Would you mind sticking around with the book until we get to a magic night? I'd kind of like to go home to the twentieth century. This may come as a surprise to you, but the book you and Angus just finished making is the same one that was in your library at home. The magic book, remember?"

Uncle Rupert's eyes grew small, then large again behind his glasses. He pulled the book out of the sack and examined it closely. He opened and began reading it eagerly, as if he were seeing it for the first time.

"Phenomenal! Remarkable! The magic of it," he murmured. "Those gray areas, those blank spaces in my memory . . ." he tried explaining to Fiona. "I see now that I couldn't remember anything that had to do with this book."

"I told you that picture of the doe was from your book, but you wouldn't believe me." Fiona pouted, remembering how unjust her uncle had been to her.

"I couldn't understand you then," protested Uncle Rupert. "The magic of the book wouldn't let me. If I had remembered the magic book, I could never have created it. It would have been a lifeless copy. Don't you see?"

"Not really," said Fiona. "But I do know that we need your book to get us home again."

"I believe tonight is one of the four magic nights, *Imbolc* Eve, when the season changes from winter to spring, a good night for time-traveling," said Uncle Rupert. "But why go home to fractions and multiplication when you could sail the seas to France?"

"There's the small matter of a frantic mother," said Fiona, beginning to lose patience with her eccentric uncle.

"Oh yes, Sadie," Uncle Rupert remembered. "You know, it occurs to me that she's just as much a McCool as the rest of us. I wonder if she could time-travel, come join us if she wanted."

Fiona smiled, thinking of the red doe. She thought of how brave Sadie had been, how she had saved them from Fear Doriche. "She probably could," she agreed. "But I happen to know she went to a lot of trouble to get us to the twentieth century, and I think we owe it to her to give it a try. How about it, Bran? Are you coming home with me?"

Fiona bit the insides of her cheeks. She wasn't going to say any more than that. She wasn't going to trick Bran into going back with her, or shame him, or tease him. Not that she didn't care if he came or not! She desperately wanted him to, and not just for Sadie's sake, but for her own sake. She had almost lost him to the Vikings, and now her heart ached to think she might lose him to another time. But let him come with her of his own free will, body and soul, or let him not come at all.

"Bran?"

Bran's head was spinning, and it wasn't only from the blows he had received. When he had first discovered Finn was his father, he had decided he would go back and take his place in the Fianna. Then he had seen Legaire fighting the Vikings and he realized that being in the Fianna would be like living in a fairy tale. He had seized the chance to be in a real battle, fighting beside his friend.

Now his friend was dead. The battle that had seemed so glorious had turned rotten and dark around him. Where in this whole world of time did he, the wizard child of Finn, belong? He stole a glance at Fiona. She had been pretty brave, for someone who was basically chicken. She had saved his life. Now that he thought of it, so had his mother. Suddenly he longed to be with the ones who loved him.

"Yeah, I'm coming," he told Fiona. "You're not too good at magic. If I let you go alone, you might end up in the middle of the ocean with Vasco da Gama or something."

Fiona wanted to cover her brother with kisses, and then she wanted to kill him for putting her through so much torture. But she did neither. Instead, she looked up at the sun. It was nearly noon. "I guess we'll have to wait till sundown for the magic to work," she said with feigned casualness. "In the meantime, does anyone have anything to eat? I'm so hungry I could eat a mouse."

"What do you suppose I had in that sack when I fled the monastery?" asked Uncle Rupert. "Besides manuscripts, I had other treasures of Clonmacnoise: a smoked ham, a loaf of wheaten bread, and a jug of that incomparable mead."

"The ham and the bread sound good," said Fiona. "But I think we'd better go easy on the mead or Bran might turn us into hedgehogs by mistake."

They all went on to the Druid grove to eat and pass the day before a warming fire. Angus sang some more songs on the harp, and each one helped ease the pain of Legaire's death.

The McCools related their adventure with Old Biddy Gwynn to Uncle Rupert, who roared when Bran described how Fiona had learned to fly. When they reached the part where Sadie had married Finn, Uncle Rupert clapped his hands.

"Marvelous! So it comes full circle. A descendant of Finn McCool marries him, renewing the magic—"

"What do you mean Finn McCool?" asked Fiona. "Did he take Ma's name when they got married? That's kind of unusual, isn't it?"

"I assumed you knew," said Uncle Rupert. "Finn was the son of Cumhall, which was once said, 'mac Cumhall.' Mac Cumhall shortens, over time, to Mac Cool or McCool. I'm amazed you two never figured out that you were descendants of Finn McCool."

Bran whistled. "This is not going to be easy to explain on my social studies homework."

"How could Ma do this to me?" wailed Fiona. "She went and married her great-great-great-great—"

"I suppose it does mean that your father and your great-great-great-ad-infinitum-grandfather are one and the same," granted Uncle Rupert. "But in a magical, mythical family such as ours, that's a minor consideration."

"I guess I'm funny that way," conceded Fiona. "Always trying to make my magic family normal. At least I'm not so afraid of the magic anymore—"

"Magic," said Bran. "I feel it getting stronger. See! The moon is up!"

A round, lemon-colored moon was balancing on the horizon, turning the oaks, in their coats of lichen, into silver Druids standing in a circle.

Uncle Rupert handed the book to Bran and kissed his niece and nephew good-bye.

"Are you sure you won't come with us?" Fiona coaxed. "It would be nice to have the whole family together again."

Uncle Rupert smiled and patted Fiona on the head. "You're young," he said. "There might even be some adventures waiting for you in the twentieth and the twenty-first centuries, but what excitement can the twentieth century hold for an aging, tenured history professor? Not much, I'm afraid."

"But, Uncle Rupert," cried Fiona, inspired, "a history professor who's traveled back in time! Just think of what you've learned! You could write books, give speeches, be on TV!"

Uncle Rupert chuckled.

"I might get on *That's Incredible*," he said. "But I'm afraid my fellow historians don't hold much with time-travelers. No, I've written history. Now let me live it."

Fiona watched her uncle's eyes dancing behind his spectacles. "He's really crazy," she thought. But he had a way of surviving, maybe because he didn't know danger when he saw it.

She gravely kissed her uncle on the cheek. "Promise me that if you get in a jam, you'll come home."

"And you promise me that if life gets boring at home, you'll come join me in the court of Charles the Bald," said Uncle Rupert. "We'd best stand out of the way,

Angus. The magic from a young Druid is apt to go a little wild."

As Angus and Uncle Rupert stepped back into the shadows, the rising moon picked out a large stone standing among the trees. It was triangular in shape, with silver lichen growing down to its middle.

"Old Biddy Gwynn!" thought Fiona as Bran began his chant. And she suddenly knew that Biddy was there to make sure they reached home safely.

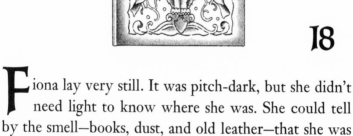

Fiona lay very still. It was pitch-dark, but she didn't need light to know where she was. She could tell by the smell—books, dust, and old leather—that she was in Uncle Rupert's library in Perry, New York.

She stood up, stumbled over to the desk, and switched on the lamp. A ragged boy was sleeping on the floor in the corner. He'd made it. He was bruised and scratched and very dirty, but he was home.

She sat down wearily at the desk and realized she was looking at Uncle Rupert's magic book. She gently touched the leather cover. It was the same cover Angus and Uncle Rupert had put on the book, but it had been through hundreds of different hands since she had last seen it.

"It's so old," she whispered. Carefully, she lifted the

cover. The book fell open to the page of the red doe. The picture didn't look at all as Fiona had remembered it. The doe was very flat, with all her feet turned one way. She stared out at Fiona with large, sad eyes.

Fiona bent over closer and examined the intricate many-colored border. There, hidden among the golden vines, were two ravens, one on either side.

Fiona turned more pages, half-hoping, half-fearing to find a picture of Sabdh, but there were none.

She jumped up and ran to look at herself in a smoky old mirror above the daybed. Same Fiona, only messier. *She* hadn't aged like the book.

Headlights swept across the mirror. A silver limousine was coming up the driveway. The car door swung open and Sadie, wearing a fur coat and blue jeans, tumbled out and ran for the house.

Fiona threw open the front door and was immediately enveloped in fur and maternal kisses.

"I'm so glad you made it! I knew you would! Such a clever girl!" Fiona heard her mother exclaiming over her head. Behind her came a uniformed chauffeur carrying a grocery bag.

"Did Bran come, too?" Sadie asked, releasing Fiona.

"He's that pile of dirty laundry snoring on the floor."

Bran staggered into the front hall.

"Bran, my poor baby!" cried Sadie. "Quick, Darin!"

She turned to the bewildered chauffeur. "We have to get this boy to the emergency ward. He's been wounded."

"I'm O.K., Ma." Bran gave his mother a hug. "All I need is a bath."

"Now I know he's sick," said Sadie. "He's never asked for a bath in his life."

Everyone laughed and Sadie calmed down enough to tell Darin to put his package in the library. She sent her children upstairs to bathe while she and the chauffeur started a fire in the library fireplace.

Bran and Fiona found some spare clothes that they kept in the rooms they used when visiting Uncle Rupert. They came down looking almost presentable.

Sadie inspected her children once again. "You need haircuts," she said. "And new clothes. You've grown. That's all right. The sales are on now."

"And dinner," said Bran. "We need food."

"Oh, of course you need food!" Sadie spread a newspaper out on Uncle Rupert's desk and began unpacking the brown bag. "How about Chinese food? Moo goo gai pan, chicken almond ding, spareribs. I bought it on the way. I figured you'd turn up here tonight, so I hired a limousine and rushed right out after the curtain call."

They sat before the fire, eating Chinese food from paper plates, laughing as Sadie caught the McCools up on all that had happened while they were away. Between bites, Fiona kept stealing glances at her mother. She was exactly the same as when Fiona had left her in October. Fiona couldn't find a trace of the red doe, or Sabdh, in that familiar face. Had it all been a dream?

Sadie sent Bran and Fiona out to the hall closet to look for old winter jackets. Darin had to check the lights on the car. Fiona stole back quietly as Sadie was feeding the paper plates, one by one, into the fire. Something in Sadie's face made Fiona stop and catch her breath. It was her eyes, large and sad. Suddenly, Fiona did see the red doe after all.

A lump came to Fiona's throat. She realized how hard Sadie had worked to make them all part of the present and how it must have hurt to leave Finn and the magic behind. How Sadie must have suffered when she realized her children had gone back. Perhaps she had even known they would go and had allowed them to take the risk!

Fiona crept to her mother's side and laid her head on her shoulder, and for a moment, each one understood what the other one knew.

"Ma," said Bran, coming in with a tweed hat that looked like an overturned pot on his head. "Can I wear Uncle Rupert's old hat? He's not coming back."

Sadie started. "Yes, I know. He—uh—left me some papers that made it pretty clear he didn't intend to—"

Bran opened his mouth to say something more, when Darin came in behind him to report that the lights were working fine.

"Terrific," said Sadie, obviously grateful to Darin for the interruption. She jumped up and pulled on her fur coat. "What are we waiting for? Tomorrow's school and I don't want you kids to miss one more day of it. Come on. You can sleep in the car."

"Sleep! Fat chance!" Bran muttered to Fiona as they went out to the limousine. "I'm going to put up that little glass window so Darin can't hear, and I'm going to ask a lot of questions."

"Bran," Fiona took her brother by the arm. "Let's give her a break, at least for tonight. She's been through a lot and now she wants to get us back to the present."

"Don't you want to know how she got back there in the first place? And what about Fear Doriche?"

"Even if we asked her, she probably wouldn't tell us," whispered Fiona, feeling wise and patient and very grown-up. "But it will all come out now that we know what to look for. We just have to keep our eyes and ears open."

"I guess you're right," said Bran, amazed to find himself agreeing with his sister. "We found our dad. That's the important part."

* * *

Sadie McCool, star of the Broadway stage, sat in the back of a silver limousine with her children on either side. Seeing they were asleep, she began humming a song to herself.

Bran and Fiona, who weren't really asleep but only faking it, winked to each other across Sadie's lap. The song had been one of Legaire's favorites.

MARY TANNEN is the author of *The Wizard Children of Finn*, also published by Knopf. "Tannen's first book reads like the work of a seasoned pro . . . an outstanding example of a book about impossibilities that are a pleasure to believe in," says *Publishers Weekly*.

Ms. Tannen was born in New London, Connecticut, and is a graduate of Barnard College. She lives in New York City with her husband, Michael, and their two children, Catherine and Noah.